tempo CHANGE

ALSO BY BARBARA HALL

The Noah Confessions

BARBARA HALL

tempo CHANGE

DELACORTE PRESS

 Published in the United States by Delacorte Press, an imprint of Random House Children's Books, a division of Random House, Inc., New York. Originally published in hardcover in the United States by Delacorte Press, New York, in 2009.

Delacorte Press is a registered trademark and the colophon is a trademark of Random House, Inc.

Visit us on the Web! www.randomhouse.com/teens
Educators and librarians, for a variety of teaching tools, visit us at www.randomhouse.com/teachers

The Library of Congress has cataloged the hardcover edition of this work as follows:
Hall, Barbara.
Tempo change / Barbara Hall.
p. cm.
Summary: Sixteen-year-old Blanche forms a band that wins a spot at Coachella, a southern California music festival, where she hopes to reconnect with her father, a famous but reclusive musician who left when she was six years old.
ISBN: 978-0-385-73607-7 (trade)—ISBN: 978-0-385-90585-5 (lib. bdg.)—
ISBN: 978-0-375-89523-4 (e-book)
[1. Bands (Music)—Fiction. 2. Fathers and daughters—Fiction. 3. Single-parent families—Fiction. 4. Fame—Fiction. 5. Coachella Valley Music and Arts Festival—Fiction. 6. California—Fiction.] I. Title.
PZ7.H1407Tem 2009
[Fic]—dc 22
2008030968

ISBN: 978-0-385-73608-4 (tr. pbk.)

Printed in the United States of America
10 9 8 7 6 5 4 3 2 1
First Trade Paperback Edition

Contents

For Faith

If we, citizens, do not support our artists, then we sacrifice our imagination on the altar of crude reality and we end up believing in nothing and having worthless dreams.

—YANN MARTEL

OPENING ACT

And So It Happened

When I got home from school there was a note by the phone.

My mother had written it. It was in her large, loopy handwriting that always seemed like it was shouting. Sometimes she actually drew flowers or smiley faces and they seemed like they were shouting, too. *Be happy! Chin up! It's all good!* But the contents were usually completely ordinary, like *Dinner's in the fridge!* or *I'll be home around eight!*

This time the note was completely different:

Maggie Somebody called from Topspin *magazine. Something about writing an article. Here's the number. She wants you to call. XOX*

I stared at it for a long time. Finally I picked up the phone and called my mom at work.

"Biscuit," she said in her chirpy tone. That was the name of the clothing store she worked in, not a nickname for me.

"Hi, Mom. What's this note?"

"What's what note?"

"Somebody called from *Topspin* magazine?"

"Oh, yes. Maggie from that magazine. I know it's a music magazine. Does this have something to do with your father? Or maybe you don't want to tell me?"

"Mom, I really have no clue. You took the call. *Topspin* is like one of the best indie magazines on the market. What about an article? Maybe it has something to do with Coachella."

"Why don't you just dial the number and see?"

"This could be a big deal," I said.

"Well, just give that Maggie a call. Let me know what she says."

I hung up and stared at the phone for another minute, then dialed the number. Someone said, "*Topspin* magazine," and I asked for Maggie and then someone said, "You got her."

"Maggie?"

"Yeah."

"This is Blanche Kelly."

"Who?"

I repeated my name. "You called about an article."

"Oh, Blanche Kelly," she said. I could hear the exhale from a cigarette. I pictured her as some hip and tortured type.

"So Blanche," she said, as if she was picking up from some conversation we had had earlier. "I'm really interested in your experience at Coachella."

"You're interested in my band, the Fringers?"

"Who?"

"The Fringers. My band. We played at Coachella. That's why you're calling? Somebody saw us there or something?"

"Everybody knows what happened there. It was history-making."

"Oh."

"And I want you to write about the whole experience."

My heart dropped a little. Deep down I'd known it would be like this. There was no escape.

"You want me to write about my father."

"Yes," she said. "That would make a great piece."

There was a protracted silence.

Then she added, "Oh, money. We pay . . ." Blah blah blah. Some words and terms that didn't mean much to me. I did some math in my head and figured out what they were going to pay me. Not that much. But this wasn't about the money.

"I'm in high school," I said.

"Right," she said.

"I'm not a professional writer."

"We know that. But we want your unique perspective."

"About my father."

"Right," she said. "You're the only daughter, right?"

I was quiet.

"You can write whatever you want. We can fix it up, you know," she added.

What could I say? That this was going to be happening to me for the rest of my life? In one way or another. While I was still quiet she piped up with "Okay, we'll pay three hundred dollars."

I was still thinking, but asked, "When would I have to deliver it?"

"I'll need it by Monday."

I laughed. "That's so soon."

She said, "I know, but that's real-world journalism."

Real world. She didn't sound too much older than me from her voice and she had figured out the real world.

"So will you do it?" she asked. " 'Cause I'll keep an open space."

"I'll think about it."

"I need it on Monday."

"Best I can say is, if you get it on Monday, then I guess you'll have your answer."

I hung up the phone and stood in the living room and thought about what I had to say.

Maggie from *Topspin* said she wanted to know about my own unique perspective. Because of my father.

As I had recently learned, it's best to be careful what you ask for.

I went into my room and turned on my computer. I stared at its blank but demanding screen. The prompter blinked.

There was so much to say.

Now I had someone to say it to.

So I started to write. I couldn't start with what Maggie called a "history-making" experience. For me it went back before that day. I started where I felt I had to . . . back to when the cracks in the dam first appeared, and then the dam burst.

SOUND CHECK

Guidance

To explain me, I'll begin with a piece of advice that my father started giving me at age three.

He said, "Blanche, don't be a joiner."

He used to say these things randomly when he was suffering through board games with me or teaching me how to play a ukulele, or at the dinner table or when he was tucking me in.

Later he said these things to me in e-mail.

E-mail allowed my father the anonymity he desired. E-mail came at you from somewhere but you didn't have to know where. My mother was one of those people who thought that these so-called technological advances were destroying community, face-to-face relationships and all that. But if it weren't for e-mail, I wouldn't have been able to talk to my father at all. And maybe that was why she hated it.

My father, see, was in hiding.

This is what he said about joining things:

"Always run as fast as you can from a big group of people and a common idea."

This philosophy had always served me well until I was sitting in my guidance counselor's office, the first week of my sophomore year at Laurel Hall Academy, under the perplexed glare of Dr. Morleymower.

"Dear Miss Kelly," he said. He was an eccentric English guy of indeterminate age. Hiring eccentric English guys was so LaHa. LaHa was the affectionate name we gave to our esteemed institution. It was kind of a joke but it was a fancy joke. Being the youngest and the worst private school in Los Angeles, they tried lots of different tricks to elevate their status. Dr. Morleymower had probably gotten his certification from the back of a magazine, but he had that accent.

"Dear, dear Miss Kelly. I'm perusing your résumé and I'm wondering what any potential university is going to make of you."

"You mean what they're going to make of my four-point-two average?"

"Well, of course, you've always performed well in the area of academics."

"I'm at an academy. I thought that was the idea."

"And yes, I find your sarcastic wit delightful, but that's not going to be reflected on your college application. You see, there will be a large space for you to list your extracurricular activities, and I'm afraid you're going to be facing a lot of white."

"I write a column for the *Manifesto*."

This was the pretentious name of our school newspaper.

"Yes, I've read your delightful column entitled 'Perspective, People.' That's correct, is it not? And in it you seem to ramble on about your disappointment in popular culture."

"It's a music column. I'm just disappointed in music."

"I'm delighted to hear that. Do you play an instrument?"

"Yes, I've played the guitar since I was six."

"My, you must be a virtuoso."

"I get around."

"And you understand theory and history and all?"

I understood history all the way back to 1955, which was more music history than most kids my age understood. I played by ear and had learned most of what I knew how to do by watching music videos and playing along with CDs. If I did say so myself, I knew my way around the guitar and had never felt the need to take classes. But I knew there was no way to impress someone named Dr. Morleymower with that.

"My training isn't formal. But neither was the training of any of my heroes. Paul McCartney can't read music."

He smiled at that, then interlaced his fingers and stared at me over the tops of his glasses.

"Do you sing?" he asked.

"Well, you know, like most people. Around the house."

"Do you perform in public? On the guitar, that is."

"No."

"So you're really just a music *fan.*"

I bristled. "I'm a music critic."

"Oh, dear," Dr. Morleymower said, and his face looked

truly stricken. Let's just say he didn't get more handsome when he did that. "Do you really think that's a worthy calling in life?"

"Somebody has to do it."

"Yes, I suppose somebody does, but it seems to me everyone rushes at that calling. 'Anti' is not actually a philosophical credo."

"Look, I can see where this is going," I said. "You want me to join some group. I'm not a joiner. And I seriously do not play sports."

"I see. Well, I'm your guidance counselor, so what good would I be if I let you cling to that position? I'm afraid I must insist you join something. I'm going to take away one of your free periods and add Madrigals to your busy schedule."

I sank into the Victorian armchair. I suspect that waves of heat were coming out of the top of my head like in cartoons. It was bad enough to join something, but a chamber choir that called itself Madrigals was just humiliating.

"I will alert Mr. Carmichael that you will be joining them for E period."

"Look," I said, "do we have to take such drastic steps? What about debate team? I'm good at arguing."

He shook his head. "You are a sophomore. By this time, most students have found their niche, and spaces are filled. We have quite a promising debate team, and there are no openings. Glancing at your options, I see the following: Equestrian. You don't happen to have a horse, do you?"

"It's a pretty small house. I think I would have noticed."

"Chess club. Do you play?"

"No, but I'm a fast learner."

"And Madrigals. Despite your denial, I suspect music is in your blood."

My spine went up, which wasn't an altogether rare occurrence for me.

"Why don't we get a blood test and see?" was my response.

Dr. Morleymower frowned and said, "Miss Kelly, if you weren't such a good student and if I were of a less sanguine disposition, I'd take offense at your tone. I might even give you a demerit. Call your mother, perhaps?"

I swallowed hard. I liked to think of myself as a rebel, but I hated getting demerits and I couldn't stand the thought of anyone calling my mother.

I looked at his watery blue eyes, and there was a deep well of determination in them. I knew I wasn't going to win this battle, so I figured I might as well take the path of least resistance.

"Madrigals," I said.

"Yes, you'll fit right in."

Fit right in.

Somewhere in the world, my father was feeling a pain deep in his chest.

You Have to Understand About My Father

He left when I was six.

I remember that day because I knew it was going to happen. It wasn't that my parents' fights had gotten louder or scarier. It was that they had stopped happening. Even as a kid I knew that was a bad thing. It meant they weren't even talking. It meant they had given up.

We lived in Silver Lake then, which was a hip part of East L.A., multiethnic and full of artists and all kinds of people with alternative lifestyles. The ladies who babysat for me next door were a couple and they were foster parents to about ten kids all of different colors, some with things wrong with them, and there were all kinds of animals, including lizards and raccoons. I loved it. I felt like I was living in a happy circus. We put on talent shows and worked in the garden and dressed the animals up in doll clothes and jumped on trampolines and there was a tree house. Somebody was always falling out of it and there were broken bones and trips to the emergency room but it all seemed normal and fun.

My house had its own kinetic energy. There were always musicians coming and going. When the musicians left, sometimes my parents would argue. Sometimes they wouldn't, they would just laugh and talk. Sometimes my father would go out to the small guesthouse behind where we lived and he'd stay there all night. That's where his studio was. I wasn't allowed to go in. Sometimes I'd peek through the dirty window and see the panels and the soundboards and the amps and the guitars and the keyboards. It looked fun but I knew it was serious.

I knew my father was famous. I just didn't know what it meant. I didn't know that famous was a rare thing to be. I thought the ladies next door—Mimi and Joss—were also famous. I thought their million kids were famous and that my mother was famous and I was, too.

When my father left, I realized that it was only him.

The musicians didn't come around anymore.

The house was quiet.

Famous had gone away.

My mother tried to soft-sell it at first. She said he was going away to think. Since I often went to my room to think, and it only took about twenty minutes, I kept expecting him to walk back in, refreshed and ready to play cards or read me a book. He sometimes did those things but it was always unpredictable. For days at a time he was in the mood for us and he'd act like a normal dad. Then he'd get a broody expression and he'd go into the studio behind the house and my mother and I would do things alone and quietly. We'd watch movies or play board games. She tried to pretend we were having normal days, but I knew we were waiting for him to come back and be cheerful. Sometimes his disappearances, or his thinking spells, would go on for what I now realize were weeks but felt like months.

When he did come back, though, it seemed like Christmas. He'd play us the songs he'd written and then his musician friends—his band, I suppose—would come over and there would be all-night jam sessions. I was able to sleep through the noise because it was happy noise. Those were exciting times, but they weren't the best times. The best times were when he was immediately finished with a project and waiting to hear from his manager or the record label, and that's when he'd play games with me and act like a dad.

Sometimes he'd go on tour with his band, and those were pretty good times, too. He was always happy when he was touring and he'd call home a lot and my mother was cheerful. Sometimes we'd fly to nearby cities to see him—San Francisco or Portland or Seattle or Las Vegas. When he came back from a tour, my mother would make him a special meal and I'd make cheesy banners and he appreciated it all for a few days, and then he'd fall into a funk and disappear.

I thought that was how all families lived. With these enormous hills and valleys, everyone tiptoeing around the unwieldy nature of talent, knowing there was a great force in the home and that force always had to be served and understood and given a wide berth. I had no idea that in some houses, most houses, every day looked pretty much the same.

I remember going to my best friend Tammy's house in kindergarten and her parents were both teachers. They came home at the same hour and they talked and they made dinner and we ate it and then we went to the den and watched television. At a certain hour, one of them would say, "Bedtime." And we'd go to bed. When we got up in the morning, they were exactly the same people they'd been the night before and there was no chance of excitement.

I felt very sorry for Tammy, and I was sure she and her family envied my family and felt inferior. Then one day Tammy and I had an argument while we were playing, and Tammy went and told her mother. I was standing outside the doorway of her shiny clean kitchen and I heard her mother say, in a low voice, "Don't be so hard on Blanche. Things are tough enough for her at home."

That was the first time it ever occurred to me that things were tough for me at home. And about to get tougher.

When my dad left, he wrote a note to my mother saying that he had to go find himself. This she explained later, not right away, and I've never seen the note, so all I have is the hand-me-down version. He said (according to her) that his priorities had gotten shifted around because of his success and he couldn't hear the music in his head anymore, and without that, he had no idea who he was.

He went around the world for a year and we'd get the occasional postcard. He finally landed in Bali and said that was where he intended to stay. He said it was a magical place and the air was clear and he could think. He sent instructions for us to join him. My mother actually started making the plans, and then she got another letter and it said, "This is no place for you two. Hang tight and I'll be home when I can."

My mother hung tight for a while and then she dropped me off at Joss and Mimi's and went to find my father. I was certain she'd be able to bring him home. She was going to pick him up, the way she picked me up from school. My mother back then was feisty and determined. She had tattoos. Small ones, where you mostly couldn't see, but this was way before anyone was doing it, let alone girls or mothers. She had short hair and it always changed colors and her eyes were green and had laughter and mischief in them. Back then. Not so much as time went on.

She didn't bring him home.

In fact, he wasn't even in Bali when she got there. He had moved on. She hadn't found him. For a long time after that, she didn't even hear from him.

It's hard to talk about the next few years. Her not leaving her bedroom. Us getting kicked out of the house. We went to live with Joss and Mimi, which felt entirely different from me just staying there during the daytime.

There was so much going on I couldn't understand. I didn't even know my mother was drinking in her bedroom and that was why she couldn't leave it.

I didn't know what had happened, either, when she suddenly got sober. Joss and Mimi, turned out, were able to help make things improve. They dragged her to AA meetings and then she started eating again and then she started talking in rhymes and slogans but she was able to leave the house and get a job.

Finally, when she moved us to Santa Monica, I felt we'd left Los Angeles altogether. Gone was the edgy feel of being in a city, the crazy loud landscape and the odd collection of people. Santa Monica was like a small town, like the one she had come from somewhere back East, and later she said she moved us there because it felt like someplace she could manage. We rented a tiny house a few blocks from Main Street and the ocean. Main Street was exactly what it sounded like, a quaint little stretch of stores and restaurants. Mom worked in a clothes store and then she became a manager. She had pulled it together (not expecting any help from my father). Eventually she opened her own place. It was called Biscuit. This clothing store took all of her time, and she said it was our future.

She decided to look into sending me to private school because she was worried about me not getting into a good college. She wanted me to have a life with choices. I took tests and scored high enough to become a scholarship kid at LaHa, and that was how my life was shaking out. LaHa wasn't a great school, Mom had a career but not really, Santa Monica was in Los Angeles but so far from it you could barely get a glimpse of the fancy life. We were on the periphery of everything.

Now that I think about it, it was probably part of the AA program that made my mother forgive my father and not say anything bad about him. She never said anything about him at all.

The last really negative thing I heard her say was on Christmas Eve when I was twelve. They had been talking on the phone and he must have made some vague commitment to come back for the holidays and then he'd backed out. She said to me, "That's just typical of your father. He never wants to have the hard conversation. He just drifts away and depends on everyone else to call it fate."

I remember lying in my bed that Christmas Eve, thinking about when I believed in Santa Claus. I mainly believed in him because my father used to put on a big show, making footprints on the carpet and creating reindeer tracks in our front yard and writing little notes from Santa on my presents. I knew he was doing it but part of me still wanted to believe. So I decided that because he, Santa, was famous, he knew my dad, who was also famous. They traveled in the same circles; they understood each other.

As I was crying in my bed that night, thinking about Santa Fraud (my new name for him), I thought also about the other big headliner of Christmas, which was God. It was all a big act. My parents didn't believe in God, really, but because they occasionally made references to Him in the early days, I bought it all. Big fat guy who brings presents, big loving Dad in the sky, why not?

Santa leaves, my father leaves, why wouldn't God leave?

My life was an evacuation site.

Wisdom from Gigi

I CAN'T TAKE YOU RIGHT INTO MADRIGALS CLASS. WE'RE going to need to stop by the lunchroom first, where I spent an hour complaining to my best friend, Gigi.

If you think this is going to be a story about how I came to love Madrigals, then keep reading. You haven't found the toy surprise.

Gigi was sitting at one of the two long Victorian tables at LaHa, studying for AP biology, even though we were three days into the semester.

Gigi was feeling a lot of pressure from her parents to become president. I'm not talking about president of the class, either. Though they were hoping for that, too. They were making her run for class office in the spring because they said any career in politics starts early. Bill Clinton, they said, was president of his class all the way through his various schools. Hillary didn't make it, but she left eighteen million cracks in the glass ceiling. Gigi was supposed to make it.

Gigi didn't talk back to her parents. They weren't that kind of parents.

She was going to be the first female minority president. She was some beautiful exotic mix of Latina, African American, and Native American. No one could be entirely sure, since Gigi was left in the parking lot of a hospital, in a basket with a note attached to her. It said: "I can't handle it."

One of the doctors at the hospital had a friend who had a friend who was Rodney Stone, a well-known real estate magnate. His face was on benches all over the city. His slogan was "Your Dream House Is Just a Stone's Throw Away." Rodney had grown sons but he had recently married his third wife, an exercise guru, who was shocked to find she couldn't have children after all those years of eating broccoli on the elliptical machine. The doctor called Rodney and Mrs. Third Wife, and that's how Gigi ended up in a mansion in Beverly Hills being groomed for president.

Gigi's full name was Georgia Erika Patterson Stone. Her mother, whose name was Erica Patterson, gave her a "k" because it seemed more ethnic. Her mother was as white as the space on my application where clubs and sports should go.

Gigi had a good attitude. She thought it was awfully big of them to rescue her in the first place and she loved them. She didn't mind being treated as if she was a project. They did it in a nice way. She knew she saved them as much as they saved her. Besides, it wasn't as if Gigi didn't have a heap of her own ambition. Her GPA was higher than mine, and that wasn't easy to pull off. She wanted it, too. She felt lucky they'd taken her in. Life was good.

Someone like Gigi belonged in one of the better private schools in L.A., like Marlborough or Harvard Westlake. The reason she wasn't was that her parents decided she would have a better chance of getting into her first-choice college if she was top of the class in a lesser-known school. I always gave them credit for thinking out of the box. She wasn't a scholarship kid, like me. She sometimes forgot that I was one and made fun of the others, who stood out a bit more. Most of the guys were on scholarship. We called them all Josh because almost all of them were actually named Josh. The Joshes were science geniuses and misfits. There were four cute guys in school, the Non-Joshes, and they were kids who were on their way to military school or detention. LaHa was the last-chance Texaco for them.

LaHa was formed by some parents whose kids couldn't get into the better schools, mainly because they'd been sent to all these experimental hippie schools all their lives, and while their self-esteem was through the roof, they had neglected to learn how to read. So LaHa was a lively mix of spoiled model types, surfers, stoners, geeks, discipline cases and brainiacs from diverse backgrounds such as myself. Gigi was a category all her own. I was an oddity because I was the daughter of someone famous, but no one really knew that. My mom totally let that go.

"Madrigals," I said. "Do you know who is in Madrigals?"

"Yes, it's all the Chelseas, Kelseys, Mercedeses, Cocos and Madisons."

This might sound hypocritical coming from a Gigi, but

to be fair, I was the only one who called her that and she pretended to loathe it.

"The actresses," I said. "The ones whose parents are going to get them into Juilliard and Carnegie Mellon and Yale."

"My parents are going to get me into Yale."

"You're going to get yourself into Yale. They just added fifteen percent more freshmen to the school. And this isn't about you."

"Sorry. Keep going."

"There won't be any guys in Madrigals."

"Who cares about guys at LaHa? Besides, isn't Josh Franklin in there?"

"No, he started wearing that surgical mask, remember, because he got so afraid of germs? You can't sing with a surgical mask."

"Oh, right. What about Josh Hammer? He's into music."

"Josh Hammer is the editor of the *Manifesto* and he knows nothing about music. Nobody here is into music, including the Madrigals. It's just an easy class."

"Maybe you'll like the singing part," Gigi said.

"I can't belong to something called Madrigals. I can't even sing."

To be honest, I had no idea whether I could really sing because I didn't try. I didn't know much about my father's singing. I couldn't listen to his music because it was upsetting to hear his voice without having a person attached to it. Sometimes I read his lyrics and I liked them. One of my favorite songs went like this:

There's a crack in the door where a little light
comes in.
I can feel the hope whispering against the wall.
But darkness is a cool and undemanding friend
And sometimes a little light is worse than none
at all.

Imagine what that guy was going through when he wrote down those words. He was an artist, no doubt about it. And it was the thing I never wanted to let myself be. That was why I was so academically inclined. And a critic. Anything was safer than art. Who wanted to feel all that pain and then write it down and spread it around?

My father always said that art was a calling, a thing that found you whether or not you wanted to be found.

But maybe he had never located a good enough place to hide.

Or maybe he had finally located it, wherever he was.

But Madrigals wasn't like being found. It was more like being forced. I chewed on a nail, thinking about it. Gigi looked up and swatted my hand away from my mouth.

"Relax. Anybody can sing in a group," she said. "Just don't sing loud."

Talking to Mom

That evening my mom knocked on my door so we could have a talk.

Imagine how excited I was about that.

I was sitting in my room listening to Fleetwood Mac on my iPod. I liked new music but I studied old music. I was obligated to understand the roots because of my job on the paper. I started going back in time that way because of my favorite contemporary bands. For example, I liked this guy named Jamie Lidell, and he said he grew up listening to Prince and Al Green, so suddenly I was listening to Prince and Al Green, and that led me all the way back to Robert Johnson, and suddenly I realized, it's all been done before. I mean, no one is going to sing "Love in Vain" better than Robert Johnson, though you have to admire the Rolling Stones for trying.

I felt it was my job to make my peers think back farther than fifth grade. "Perspective, People" was the name of my column. Some people loved it, some people hated it, and I kept the letters editor in business.

So I was listening to Fleetwood Mac because I had been hearing Lindsey Buckingham–style guitar in lots of modern songs and I wanted to talk about that. Basically, there wouldn't be any sensitive guys with acoustic guitars playing today if it weren't for Lindsey Buckingham. I was thinking of starting my column that way.

I was trying to wipe off the disaster of being assigned to Madrigals.

But first my mother with the knock and the talk.

She stood in the doorway with a fake smile acting like she just wanted to make sure I was studying. The grades concern was always her way in. I think my mom wasn't all that sure of how to be a mother since day one. I had limited information about her childhood and less about my grandmother. Mom kept all that to herself. She'd been in survival mode since Dad left. When she got sober, it was like she had another kid named Sobriety and Sobriety was a lot more high-maintenance than I was and needed a lot more attention. I was the kid who never got in trouble. I never did get in trouble but I always looked like I might.

For example, I dyed my hair red. Which wasn't all that strange except that my hair was red. Now it was growing out and it was two different shades of red. I frosted the tips blond. I had the hair of a troubled kid.

Mom was all excited when Laurel Hall Academy formed and actively started recruiting smart kids from public schools. Even though I didn't mind the gigantic Oceanside High School I attended, it was a little too close to the bad part of Venice and there had been some incidents of violence, and drugs were everywhere. Mom trusted me to resist all that, but at the end of the day, I think she lost her nerve because she remembered what she was like at my age. She wasn't like me. She didn't just have the hair of a troubled kid. She was one.

I had memories of my mom being kind of artsy and loose and funny when I was young. Later she told me the word for that was "drunk." Now that she was in the program, she was more solid, but it was like that solidness had taken over everything and she didn't have a past that she owned. She didn't admit, even to herself, that there had been some good times when Dad was around.

Now what she was, was reliable. She worked all the time. Her idea of socializing was meeting some of her AA friends at the Fig Tree on the beach for endless pots of tea. They talked about other AA members and people they might have to intervene on and all that. She was constantly helping. When she wasn't helping she was talking about the clothes at Biscuit, the inventory, the sales figures, the money, the money, the money. She worried about it all the time. Not to me but on the phone with her sponsor.

Talking about the Money was a way of talking about Dad. He had left us without any to speak of. It's not that we were ever rich, she explained to me. Even when Dad was making money he didn't know how to handle it and somehow it just disappeared. So Mom knew a thing or two about how to live paycheck to paycheck. She had bought our tiny house with some savings he had freely given over to her when he walked out. He sent us money sporadically—big and small checks coming at random times, like Christmas out of nowhere.

Not having money was not a thing I worried much about, even at LaHa. In fact, at LaHa I kind of wore it like a badge. My father was always a little proud of his financial difficulties. In fact, sometimes he admitted that the money was what drove him away from his calling. He remembered a time when making music had nothing to do with making money. And when the checks rolled in, he felt it was a kind of betrayal.

In my research for the column, I once read that the money was what did in Kurt Cobain (of Nirvana fame). He couldn't reconcile the popularity with the purity of the art. And so the shotgun to the head. Reinforcing my belief that being an artist made it nearly impossible to be anything else, including, sometimes, alive.

But back to my mother in the doorway.

"Did you eat anything?" she asked.

It was always what she asked when she came into my room. It was as if someone had given her a manual that told her what questions to ask her teenager.

"No."

"Blanche, you have to eat."

"I ate at school. I had yogurt on the bus. I don't have anorexia. My grades are fine."

"I know that."

"I don't smoke, drink or do drugs or have sex."

"Is that funny to you?"

"No, Mom. Nothing much is funny to me."

"Well, I don't want you to be that way."

"What way do you want me to be?"

"Happy, Blanche."

"I'm fine."

"I know, I know, everything is fine with you."

"Then what's the problem?"

The question was a mistake. It gave her an opening to come all the way into the room and sit on my bed. She was wearing a tie-dyed tank and a denim skirt and flip-flops and lots of jewelry from head to toe. She was tanned. Her hair was a shade darker than mine naturally was, and French New Wave short while mine was retro-hippie long, and she didn't wear makeup. She knew exactly who she was all the time, even if she didn't know what she was doing. When she didn't know what she was doing, that was who she was—a person who didn't know what she was doing. Which is to say my mother had forgotten how to be fake, if she'd ever known. Being honest was a very big part of the program. She was committed to this.

This is what I knew. She started out in L.A. as a girl fresh off the bus from a New England town she didn't like to talk about. She came to L.A. to be famous even though she didn't know what she'd do to become famous. She painted some and modeled some and acted some. But mostly she went to parties. At a concert at the Troubadour she met my dad, who was on his way to being famous. They got married. Mainly because of me. While Dad was on his way to being famous, she worked in a lot of crazy jobs, from yoga and meditation teacher to massage therapist to exotic dancer—something she still didn't like to discuss, like the small town in New England. Since my mother had gotten sober and serious about living, she didn't want to think about all the time she'd spent wandering.

I knew not to ask about her family. I knew even less about my father's early life. Their parents were either dead or not talking to them. They only had each other, she told me. That was a thing they had in common. Being all alone in the world. Until they found each other.

She sat on my bed. "It worries me," she said, "that you don't have many friends. You're isolated. It's a dangerous thing to do to yourself."

"I am not isolated. I have a friend."

"You need more than one. Gigi is a good person, but you can't expect her to be everything. You need people, Blanche. We all act like we can do things alone but we can't."

"Mom, I'm not in the program."

"This isn't the program talking. It's me."

"Don't mention God, okay? Because I seriously cannot go there right now."

"I'm not talking about any of that. This is just a normal mother wanting to see her kid have a social life."

"Most normal mothers just want their kids to get good grades."

"I want to see a balance."

"Do I follow you around and demand to see a balance? All you do is work and go to meetings."

She thought for a moment, then said slowly, "It worries

me because I see you doing some things that are like your father."

"I do have his genes. Why does it worry you?"

"Because of how he ended up—lost and unhappy."

Actually, she didn't know how he ended up. I couldn't tell her that I did. Technology changed things. She didn't know that he was living on an island in Hawaii. He was driving a taxi during the day and writing songs at night. He was going to record them himself. He didn't need the outside world telling him how to make music. I was the only person in the world who knew that. Because of the e-mails.

"What are the things you see me doing?"

"You stay in your room," she said, "and play music."

"I do other things."

She raised an eyebrow at me.

"Mom, would it help you to know that I'm being forced to join the chamber choir at school? I mean, it's music, but it's not isolating."

"Really?" she said, and I couldn't tell if that made her feel better or not.

"And I have a job. That's something."

"I know," she said.

She was staring at my guitar case. It was my father's old guitar. A Gibson J45 with a crack on the top, but it sounded amazing.

She said, "It's even his guitar."

"Right."

"I wouldn't be surprised if he wanted it back someday. It's probably worth something."

"He's not going to want it back."

"You don't know him," she said.

It was true I didn't know him very well. But I knew him better than she thought.

We never talked about my communicating with him. I didn't know if she knew or not. It didn't matter as long as we never discussed it—that was my attitude.

I said, "Mom, why don't you stop worrying? You work hard enough all day. Why don't you meet Louise for some tea at the Fig Tree? I am fine."

"I want you to be better than fine, Blanche, I want you to be happy." She looked at her watch. "I guess I'll go meet Louise. She'll want to talk about her married boyfriend."

"Why doesn't she go back to drinking? I mean if she's just going to do stupid stuff."

Mom said, "Her thing wasn't alcohol. It was cocaine. Now she just starves herself and dates unavailable men."

"I thought when you get sober you're supposed to give up stupid."

"No, you just give up substances. Stupid hangs around."

"Really, Mom. Go out."

"Okay," she said.

"I'm so glad we had this talk, which got us nowhere. See you later, Mom."

"I just chip away at the wall," she said. "One day I'll break through."

"God loves you for trying," I said.

She blew me a kiss and went out.

I pulled out this scrapbook that my mom had kept when she and my dad were still together and he was starting to get famous. She had thrown it out when we moved but I found it in the trash and took it and had kept it hidden in my room ever since.

For two years in a row, a famous critics' poll had listed my father as the top artist of the year. This was the year I was born and the year after. In the pictures of him he is sullen and serious. He is a skinny, wiry guy; his hair is all over the place, and he's always carrying that cracked Gibson and staring anywhere but right at the camera.

In one picture, he's in the house in Silver Lake and my mother and I are in the background. You can barely see us. We're shadows. She's wearing a halter dress and lots of jewelry and I'm slung over her shoulder, and all you can see about me is how wide my eyes are, like I'm completely shocked by my life.

My father is staring, his chin propped on his fist, as if he's just dreaming us.

Madrigals

I STOOD IN A CORNER OF THE CLASS, PRETENDING I WASN'T really supposed to be there. I listened to the inane chatter of the Chelseas and Madisons, talking about how they would die if they didn't get a solo in the upcoming auditions.

I didn't say anything. I just stared at my text messages. My text file was empty but I stared anyway. Every one of the girls in Madrigals was destined for greatness because of their parents' or their parents' friends' proximity to the entertainment industry.

No one knew about my connections. They didn't because I didn't want them to. Not that they would have heard of my father. People in Madrigals didn't know what had happened in music two years ago, let alone fourteen.

Music nerds knew who my father was. They were enthusiastic about him but they were smallish in number. Except on the Internet, where you could find entire Web sites devoted to him—his work, along with trivia and so-called sightings. I checked in every now and then but forbade myself to log on. I enjoyed being a spectator.

I had decided long ago that I wouldn't trade on my father's fame. Then again, how could I? He wasn't famous anymore. He had dropped out of society at the height of his popularity. For a while that was the thing that made him famous, all the speculation about what happened and when he was coming back and if he was dead, had lost his mind, changed into a woman, every imaginable scenario. After a while, though, other people got famous and did crazier things, like Jeff Buckley jumping into the water with his boots on or Kurt Cobain going wild on drugs and fame and killing himself or Paul Westerberg drinking himself off the map or Elliot Smith stabbing himself in the heart. My father's moving to a tropical island just didn't rank up there with the rock disasters.

My mother worried about the fact that I had his genes. She thought it was the art that made him crazy, not that he was an artist who went crazy. But she also had this part of her brain that still believed in him. She'd hear a song on the radio and say, "Your father invented what they're doing. Right there, that riff? That thing? He invented it."

She didn't really know how to talk about music but she knew when he had invented it. That was ironic to me. I said nothing.

Mr. Carmichael came into the room. Mr. Carmichael had a sad and lethargic look. He had a weepy-looking goatee, and earrings in both ears, but was otherwise the picture of normality. He sat down at the piano and approached it as if it were a wounded patient he needed to revive, and his efforts to revive said wounded patient mostly ended in disappointment. He was, I'd have to guess, forty, and he carried around with him some kind of desperately lost ambition.

He said, "Okay, girls, let's calm down and talk about music."

The Madrigals scattered into order and I was the only one left standing, not knowing where to turn.

Mr. Carmichael turned to me. He said, "Are you the latest addition? Blanche Kelly?"

"Yes," I said.

"Are you a soprano?"

"I don't know."

"Well, stand on the riser next to Viv and we'll figure it out."

That's when I met Viv. I stood on the riser next to her.

Viv barely glanced at me and I barely glanced at her.

As far as I knew, Viv Wyler was the soccer goalie. I had no idea that she had any musical interest, let alone aspirations. She was tall and boxy and full of muscles that I'd assumed only boys had. She was pretty, but she had no grace and apparently no sense of humor. I had never seen her smile, let alone laugh. She had long, blond, unkempt athlete's hair and a bland face.

I looked at her but she stared straight ahead. I knew she was a bad student. At LaHa, you got to know the bad students. Rumor had it that her parents were scholars and scientists; she had two sisters who were on their way to being astrophysicists; and she somehow had the brains of a nylon rope. To the degree that she had a name for herself, she had made it in front of the soccer net. Her parents were hoping that her soccer accomplishments could at least get her into a state college.

I tried to smile at her but her eyes just flitted across me and went back to the center of the room.

Mr. Carmichael started playing "Fire and Rain," an old James Taylor song, and I just jumped right in since I knew it. At first I wasn't sure what that beautiful sound was, that elegant tone and tight vibrato. I looked all over the room and it sounded like it was coming from me, which I knew was impossible. Then I realized it was coming from right next to me.

Viv Wyler had a beautiful voice.

Mr. Carmichael stopped playing piano and looked straight at me.

"Blanche, aren't you singing the alto part?"

"What?"

"You're singing with the altos."

"Oh."

"So step up a level."

I did. The Chelseas made room for me. But I couldn't stop staring at Viv. She saw me staring at her and I looked away. Madison raised her hand and said, "Mr. Carmichael, can we sing something else? This is like a hundred years old."

"We're singing James Taylor," the beleaguered Mr. Carmichael said, wiping his brow.

I said out loud for all to hear, "You know this song is about a friend of his who died in an airplane crash."

"No way," the girls crooned.

"Really. Sweet dreams and flying machines in pieces on the ground."

The girls started mumbling. Mr. Carmichael gave me an appreciative smile.

"From the top," he said, and we stumbled our way through it.

When the class was over, Mr. Carmichael made an announcement.

"School talent competition is a month away. I'm accepting applications now. Please list the song you'll be performing, all participants, and all instrumentation."

Everyone stared at him.

It wasn't that kind of school.

The bell rang and we filed out. I couldn't help catching up to Viv.

"Hey," I said. "You have a great voice."

She looked at me. "So?"

I shrugged. "I don't know. I thought I'd tell you that."

"What good will it do me? Is it going to get me into college?"

"Maybe."

"This is an easy A. That's all it is to me."

"But you could actually be a singer or something."

She slowed down her soccer player's lope and stared at me. "I read your column. I know you care a lot about music. What I can't figure out is why."

"Because it's . . . I'm . . . What else is there?"

"Soccer," she said. "And trying to keep my head above

water to make my parents happy. That's all I can handle right now. But thanks for the compliment."

She hurried down the carpeted hallway to her next class. I could feel an idea forming in my brain like a storm cloud. Like a crack of light under the door.

Sometimes a little light is worse than none at all.

Peace Pizza

WORK. THAT'S WHAT I DID AFTER SCHOOL AND ON THE WEEK-ends. While the other girls from LaHa were hanging out at the Promenade or the Pier or Amoeba Records in Hollywood or the Abercrombie at the Grove or the Arclight Theaters. Working in their spare time was something poor kids did.

I worked at Peace Pizza. Only in Santa Monica would a pizza restaurant name itself that with no irony whatsoever. The owner, Toby Myerson, was a burnout from the seventies who had never gotten over Amnesty International and Greenpeace. The place was full of signs that said things like "Love Is All You Need" and "Be Good to Your Mother—Earth." Toby rode a bike and wore hemp clothing and meditated a lot. He only showed up at the store late in the evenings, usually stoned. So the whole place was basically run by a bunch of teenage surfer dudes. The oldest guy there, the assistant manager, was Jeff, a lanky nerd who ran track and jumped over stuff at Pali High, a public school in the Palisades. He was a junior and he was smart, I could tell, because he was always hitting his books between customers and I knew the colleges he was applying to—Stanford, MIT, and Northwestern. I'd heard he wanted to be an engineer but I didn't know what kind.

Jeff was always wrangling the younger guys, the Seans and the Bos and the Tylers, trying to get them to do something other than yak about surfing and skateboarding. When they did that, all the work fell on Jeff's shoulders and mine, and sometimes on the snarly cook, Ella, who had to jump in and work the cash register. That was never a good plan because she didn't have much in the way of people skills. She looked like a boy and didn't mind people making that mistake. Other than the fact that she cooked really fast, I didn't know much about her.

Jeff and I always took our breaks together and we talked about music. He had great taste and he was the only person I knew who could talk music history. He could get from Jimmie Rodgers to the Beatles to U2 in three steps. I liked that in any person. I wondered why he couldn't put on a few pounds. But it was none of my business.

It was shortly after Madrigals, and we were sitting on the picnic bench outside of work, when he said to me, out of nowhere, "Hey, Street, I heard a rumor that your father was Duncan Kelly. That guy from the nineties who invented the whole grunge movement before its time."

He called me Street because my name was Blanche. I

didn't mind the nickname. Get it? *Streetcar Named Desire*, Blanche DuBois. That was engineering-geek humor.

"It wasn't grunge," I said. "It was more like hard acoustic."

"What?"

"He played acoustic guitar but it wasn't, you know, soft. It rocked. And the lyrics were smart."

"Like Paul Westerberg or something?"

I had to admit, I was impressed that he knew who that was. Paul Westerberg was a guy about my dad's age who had a band called the Replacements who were poppy and punk at the same time. My dad was a little like that, only more moody and less poppy.

"Not exactly like Westerberg. They were contemporaries."

"Did he know him?"

"Jeff," I said, "who told you about my father? How can a geek like you care about music? Aren't you going to build bridges or rockets or something?"

"Just because I'm good at math doesn't mean I can't like music. Now, come on, Street, answer my question."

"Yeah, that's my dad."

"Wow. So do you know where he is and stuff?"

"Not really, she lied."

"Why don't you ever tell anybody?"

"I'm not supposed to know where he is. He doesn't want anyone to know."

"I mean that you're related to him."

"Who would I tell?"

"You could have told me."

"Nobody cares who he is anymore."

"I care who he is."

"You're weird."

"I've heard his music, too. That record *Ineffable*, that's a seminal record."

I looked down and blushed. Suddenly it made me feel weird to think of anyone other than me listening to my father's music. Someone I actually knew.

Even though I teased him about being a geek, I knew Jeff's iPod was the envy of everyone. It's the one we always plugged into the system when we were working.

Jeff was one of those people who collected music, and the information about it, as if it were baseball cards or stamps. He didn't try to play it himself. He thought knowing about it somehow got him in the club. I knew I was in danger of becoming exactly that kind of person. Writing *about* music wasn't the same as writing it. I intended to correct that about myself one day. Just as an exercise, to prove I could do it. A pastime, not a way of life.

Well, the truth was, I had already started the process. I had contraband under my mattress.

Not weed or a flask or even something worse. What I had tucked away was pages and pages of what I liked to call poetry. Teenage girls were expected to write poetry. But really they were songs. Words waiting for notes. I was as ashamed of it as another girl might be about pornography. It was the thing I didn't want to know about myself and certainly never wanted my mother to know. That in my most rebellious, secretive hours, I was practicing something dangerously close to art. I thought if I never told anyone, it didn't have to be true. I figured I'd never tell anyone but maybe someday someone would find all that stuff, the way someone found Emily Dickinson's trunks of poetry long after she was dead. That seemed like an okay plan to me. To be an artist after you were dead. Let someone else give me that label. I'd never own it myself.

"So he's really still alive, then?" Jeff asked about my father.

"He's alive."

"In prison?"

I laughed and spit out my Diet Coke.

"No, in a yurt or something. He's finding himself."

"How long does something like that take?"

"So far about a decade. He left when I was little. I don't know, it's some kind of vision quest. He can't explain it well, so I can't, either."

"You live with your mom, then?"

"Yeah."

"You ever hear from him?"

"All the time. We e-mail." I couldn't believe I'd just said that.

"That's good," he said. He stared off and then lit a cigarette.

I glared at him but he just kept smoking, daring me to say something.

I wasn't a stranger to cigarette smoke. Lots of my mom's friends smoked because they were sober and somehow you were allowed to hold on to that vice. She didn't let them smoke in the house but they were always in the backyard, puffing away. I thought it was so strange how some vices were off-limits while others were not so bad and it all depended on what crowd you ran with.

I added, "Hey, listen, don't tell anyone that I talk to my dad. Not even my mother knows."

I had only given him half the story. My father and I did e-mail but not regularly. I waited to hear from him the way I imagined normal girls would wait to hear from an aloof guy they liked.

"I don't know my dad," Jeff said, puffing.

"Where does he live?"

"I don't know. He took off like yours did."

"Wait, mine didn't just take off for no reason. He's finding himself. He's an artist."

"Okay," he said.

"He had vision and purpose. The whole fame thing got to him. So he left."

"About ten years ago."

"Right." I let a minute pass and then I said, "Jeff, how can you smoke? You're a big track star."

"I'm a walking contradiction," he said.

He was quiet and I let him be. It made me nervous but my father also told me it was important to let silence accumulate. People thought they had to fill the gaps all the time. But it was important, in singing as well as relationships, to allow for space.

Not that Jeff and I had a relationship. Talking to him was okay. I used him for practice.

He looked at me. I looked at him.

Jeff had great hair. It was thick and it fell into his face

and he shook it out. He must have known he looked cute when he did that.

"What about you? Are you musical?" he asked.

"I play the guitar a little."

He nodded, looking at the cigarette more than smoking it. He jerked his head back toward the kitchen.

"Ella's a drummer, you know."

"What?"

"And she goes to your school. She's good, too."

"What?"

"Laurel Hall. That's you, right?"

"I've never seen her there."

"Maybe you never looked."

I stared through the glass and saw her pulling a pepperoni pizza out of the oven as gingerly as if she were delivering a baby. Then she slammed it on the counter and hit the bell.

"If I did see her, I must have thought she was a guy."

"Laurel Hall has guys?" Jeff asked.

"Not really. They just have some people who aren't girls."

Jeff laughed.

"You're funny," he said.

"Thanks."

"Funny girls aren't usually pretty."

"Is that the case?"

"Well, pretty girls aren't usually funny."

"Is this your gearheaded way of giving me a compliment?"

"Whatever," he said, and he was blushing. As much as I

was a loner, I'd found it wasn't hard to make guys do that. I knew that I was different and some guys liked that. Once it was clear that a guy was even remotely interested, all you had to do was call them on it to see what they'd look like with a pink complexion.

"Maybe it's a sign," Jeff said. His face was working its way back to pale.

"What?"

"The fact that Ella is a drummer and goes to your school and works here."

"Sign of what?"

"I don't know, Street. Help me out here."

"I don't believe in signs."

"You don't?"

"My dad told me to beware of things that a lot of people believe."

"He's probably right about that," Jeff said.

"So if you believe in signs, you probably believe in God," I said.

"No, not really."

"Because you're not going to get anywhere with me, talking about God. I get too much of it at home."

"Your mother is religious?"

"AA," I said. "There's a lot of God talk but it's vague. God of your understanding and all that."

"It doesn't rub off on you?"

"God is not understandable to me."

"Well, isn't that the point?"

"I don't know what the point is, Jeff."

"I think it's pretty obvious there's some kind of plan. A

scheme, a system. Numbers have taught me that. All those X's and O's. You don't have to know what the system is to understand it. I mean, the idea that we keep inventing systems, algorithmic and whatnot, means we're modeling it after something that already exists."

"You're losing me."

"We'll pick this up tomorrow," he said. "So little time, so many pizzas to make."

Right before I punched out, I got up my nerve and approached Ella. I didn't think she and I had said more than twelve words to each other in the whole year we'd both been working at Peace. Which was why I didn't know she went to Laurel Hall. She was shoving a pizza into the oven and her back was to me but somehow she saw me anyway.

"What do you want?" the back of her head said to me.

"Oh, I just wondered . . . I was thinking . . . I'm Blanche."

"You're thinking you're Blanche?"

"I know I am."

"I know you're Blanche, too."

"Well, we've never actually talked."

"Eight people work here. Two are girls. I figured it out."

"Okay. So I just found out you go to LaHa?"

"Yep."

Still with her back to me.

"I go there, too," I said.

"You are telling me things I know. Do you want to explain prime numbers or gravity next? I'm working."

"I write the music column."

She turned. Her face was small and fierce. Her dark eyes

were piercing and her hair was almost short enough to be considered a buzz cut. She reminded me of Sinead O'Connor, who was an Irish singer famous for a Prince song called "Nothing Compares 2 You." She got even more famous by tearing up a picture of the pope on *Saturday Night Live*.

"I've read your column," Ella said. "You know a lot about old music. You've got a lot of opinions, too."

"Oh, thanks."

She shrugged. "It seems like a waste of time."

I said, "Why do you go to LaHa? I'm a scholarship kid."

She stared at me for a while.

"I got kicked out of all the others."

"What for?"

"Breaking the rules. Being weird. Who knows."

"Jeff said you play the drums?"

She shrugged. "I fool around."

"Well, I need a drummer."

"What for?"

"I've been thinking about something. I thought I'd run it by you."

She waited.

"Okay?" I asked.

"I'm waiting."

"I want to start a band."

The sentence came out, just like that. I was startled myself. I wanted to put it all the way back in my mouth and down my throat. It was the scariest thing I'd ever said out loud. But the idea was finally taking over me and I knew there was no going back. Research, I told myself. Experience, not art.

Her expression didn't change.

"Covers?" she asked.

"Well, no. I would want to do original stuff."

"You write the songs?"

I gulped.

"Yes. Well, I fool around with lyrics. I'm more interested in the music. Performing. I need some stuff on my résumé."

She ignored this fumbling and I was grateful.

"Who sings?" she asked.

"I'm working on that."

"Find a singer," she said. "And get back to me."

She pulled a pizza out of the oven and started slicing it into pieces.

You would not want to be that pizza.

The Fringers

I CAN'T KEEP YOU IN SUSPENSE ABOUT THE BAND COMING TOGETHER. It did.

The way I got this to happen was pretty much the same way I got myself to keep up an above-four-point average. I put myself out on a limb. I made sure that it mattered more than anything. I took classes that were almost too hard and I had something enormous to lose if it didn't come together. I'm aware there are people who motivate themselves normally but this has always been my approach. Head on the chopping block.

My father once told me that the difference between people who succeeded and those who didn't was willingness. He wrote music because he was willing. My mother believed the opposite. She was powerless. She surrendered to the God of her understanding and He told her to work in a clothing store. Willingness had bigger plans for me. And what made a person willing? I didn't know that.

Something told me I could not just be someone who talked about music.

I wrote my last column of "Perspective, People." It was a bit of a diatribe about Fleetwood Mac, encouraging everyone to go back and discover them. In the last paragraph I announced that I was going to take a little time off to pursue my own musical aspirations with my band the Fringers, which consisted of myself, Vivien Wyler on vocals, Georgia Stone on keyboards, and Ella Tandy on drums.

The article came out and I sat and waited in the lunchroom to be assaulted by my fellow band members.

I had taken this approach because of something else my father once said to me. He said, "If you want to make a thing happen, say it is so, and then keep your word."

Viv, Gigi, and Ella found me at roughly the same time in the lunchroom and they stood around me in a semicircle of glares. The article had the desired effect. They had seen it in print and now it had to be true.

"What are you talking about?" Gigi shrieked. She got very shrieky when anyone interrupted her carefully scheduled future plans. "We aren't in a band."

"We could be, though. It'll be good for us," I said.

"Good for us how?" she demanded.

"And what us?" Viv asked. "I barely know you guys."

Ella just glared and chewed on a thumbnail. Because of her silence, I knew she was already adjusting to the idea. Glaring was her natural state, anyway.

I explained. I said we didn't have to stay together forever, but I thought we should put a band together and enter the talent show.

"The talent show?" Viv exclaimed. "Nobody takes the talent show seriously."

"But the winners of their school talent shows automatically qualify for High School Band Night at the Whisky."

High School Band Night was a pretty well-known affair. Because we lived in L.A., teens who played in bands were taken very seriously. They were surrounded by the music industry—agents, managers, always scouring the city for the next big thing. Kids in L.A. attended High School Band Night at the Whisky the way kids in other cities attended the prom or football games.

"What's the upside of it?" Viv asked. "I have to have an answer because my dad always wants to know what the upside of stuff is."

"My parents will want to know how it's going to look on my college résumé," Gigi agreed.

I looked at Ella, who was still just glaring at me, chewing on the nail.

"What are your issues?" I asked.

"Who says I have issues? I just don't like finding out I'm in a band by reading it in the school paper."

"You told me to find a singer and get back to you. Well, I found the singer."

I smiled at Viv and she looked away.

"I don't know if I can just sing in front of people like that," she said. "I'm used to singing in a large group."

"Why am I playing keyboards?" Gigi asked.

"Because you've had piano lessons since you were a kid."

"I play Beethoven. And what are you going to do, drag a piano onto the stage?"

"I don't know. An electric keyboard. We'll figure it out. The important thing is, we're a band."

They got quiet and thought about it. While they were thinking about it, the headmistress of LaHa, Dr. Bonny, came by. She was a smiley woman in colorful power suits with a strong addiction to Altoids. She chomped them nervously, and behind her eternal smile was this forced quality that I thought revealed a sense that LaHa was always on the verge of falling apart.

She said, "Girls, congratulations. Such a talented group of people here at Laurel Hall. I commend you. The Fringers. That's a wonderful name. That's . . ."

She walked off, still talking, which was another thing she always did.

The Fringers were still staring at me.

"For you, Gigi, a no-brainer. It makes you look well-rounded. Ivy Leagues love that," I said.

"Keep talking," Viv said.

"It's good for your lungs, singing. Good for your body, too. It'll help when it's time to play soccer. What is that, a winter sport?"

"Yep."

"The talent show will be over by then. The Whisky is right before winter break."

They considered it. I saw them falling for it, so I just waited.

Finally Gigi said, "The Fringers? That's what we're called?"

"Sure. I mean, LaHa, it's a fringe school. We'll be competing with the established schools. It's a celebration of the underdog."

Ella stopped chewing her nail and said, "I kinda like that."

"What are we going to play?" Gigi asked.

"I'm writing something. You'll like it."

"You write music?" Gigi asked. She was staring as if she were seeing me for the first time.

"Where are we going to rehearse?" Ella asked. "I play loud."

"Peace Pizza. I asked Toby and he says we can use the banquet room after nine o'clock if nobody's in there."

"Nobody's ever in there," Ella said. "Nobody has pizza banquets."

The bell rang. Viv and Ella walked away talking about how they'd get to Main Street, what bus they'd take, or if one of Viv's sisters could drive them.

Gigi was still standing there.

She said, "It's a dirty trick, Blanche. You know that, don't you?"

"It's not a trick. It's a plan."

"It's a dirty plan."

"You're going to thank me," I said. "Just wait."

She shook her head but she walked away smiling.

When I went home that night, after work, I found the living room of our house full of Twelve Steppers. They were drinking tea and one of them was crying and the rest were all hanging on her every word. The crier wasn't Louise. In fact, Louise wasn't there, which was unusual. Maybe she had a date with the married man.

My mother looked up at me and asked if everything was all right. I said it was. She went back to listening.

I checked my e-mail and there was nothing from my father. But I didn't expect it. They were few and far between. I had already gotten a couple this month so I wasn't due for a while. Sometimes I could get him to respond by telling him something new or asking him a question. So I sat down and e-mailed him:

> Hey, Dad,
> Just checking in. School is school and L.A. is the way it always is, full of sunshine and promises. I've started a band called the Fringers and we're working hard to get our act together in time for the talent show. The talent show at LaHa is lame but if we win, we get to play at the Whisky. I'd appreciate any tips you have.

I stared at what I'd written and then I hit Send and I felt that message traveling through the system, the whirring mass of X's and O's that Jeff talked about, the perfect system mimicking some bigger system that I didn't believe in, but like everyone else, I believed in this one. This tiny thread that kept me connected to him. I swear, I could feel it when my words landed.

FIRST SET

Rehearsal

WHEN YOU DECIDE TO START A BAND, NO ONE TELLS YOU (AND you certainly don't think about it) that you are going to end up being a kind of substitute teacher. No one wants to listen to you because they don't recognize you as an authority figure. You're one of them. You can't possibly know what you're doing.

A lot of things happened that I hadn't counted on. First, Gigi decided to play bass instead of keyboards. The idea came to her when her father, Rodney Stone, said he was a bass player in college and wouldn't it be fun for her to learn his instrument? He didn't have his instrument anymore so he'd gone out and bought a brand-new one for her. He'd also bought her a bass amp. Then he bought us a guitar amp and a PA system. I suddenly saw the benefits of having rich friends. On the other hand, it meant that the pressure was on. Adults were invested. Rodney wanted to hang around for rehearsal, but Gigi convinced him that most rock stars didn't have their parents hanging around rehearsals. Her mother, Erica with a "C," made us T-shirts with our names on them and some business cards. This was all before we'd learned one song, so I definitely felt we couldn't back out now.

Gigi was a little surprised at her parents' sudden acceptance of this new venture, and I had to admit that I was, too. I thought rebellion was supposed to be part of it somehow but everyone approved. Almost everyone. More on that later.

Our first rehearsal took place in the banquet room of Peace. Nine o'clock, after the rush.

Off the bat, there was the problem that even though she had a brand-new amp and a bass guitar, Gigi didn't actually know how to play bass. I didn't know how to teach her, either. Ella could get her to follow along with the beat she was creating on the drums, but when Ella tried to deviate with some frills or anything fancy, Gigi would lose her way. I struggled to show her what to do but it really wasn't my instrument. I was talking about eighth versus quarter notes when Viv spoke up. She said, "It's kinda like a voice, you know. Like a backing vocal, you know? Like in a song when someone is going 'bop bop bop' in the background. You're the bop bop."

This is what worked.

Then everybody had thoughts on my song. I certainly hadn't counted on that.

The song was called "Walking Contradiction." Okay, I

had written it about Jeff but I hoped he'd never figure that out. Guys mostly didn't listen to lyrics.

It went like this:

He has short blond hair and a penetrating gaze.
He's got petal red cheeks and a cigarette haze.
He's got plans for the future, he's gonna program your world.
He's got eyes for everything except a girl.
He wants to fall in love, yeah, he's got that predilection
But he's just a walking contradiction.

"What's a predilection?" Viv asked. "I don't know what that is. I can't sing it if I don't know what it is."

"It's a tendency."

"I don't get it. First you say he doesn't see the girl and then you say he wants to fall in love."

"Yeah, Viv, it's a contradiction."

"Who's this about?" Gigi asked.

"Jeff," Ella said. "The assistant manager out there."

I felt overwhelmed with embarrassment.

"No, it's not."

"Sure it is."

"It's not about him. That's not how songwriting works. Now, it's in the key of G and let's figure out a tempo."

"G, really?" Gigi frowned. "It's such a happy key."

"It's the people's key. Tempo."

Ella gave us one and Gigi said it was too fast and Ella

said it wasn't, she was too slow, and the Bos and Seans and Tylers hung around the door and giggled at us until I shooed them away.

And then we all started throwing ideas out until everybody was on the same page and we did one version of the song where we got all the way through and it didn't suck. By then it was midnight.

Jeff was waiting for me outside when we left. Gigi and Viv took the bus and Ella rode her bike in the opposite direction. Gigi and Viv had been talking in a very animated way, and I noticed that Gigi was a lot more relaxed than I had ever seen her. Viv had a glow to her, too. The band was good for everyone but me. I felt exhausted.

"Three hours, one song. Pretty good," Jeff said.

"Don't start." I collapsed on the curb beside him.

"No, I mean, it sounded pretty good."

"I don't know how we're going to get there. We'll be all right for the talent show but if we're going to get into the Whisky show, we have to have a bunch of originals."

"Then I guess I'll have to keep inspiring you."

"That song is not about you," I said.

He smiled.

"You do it the way anything gets done," he said. "One foot in front of the other."

"Is that gearhead wisdom?"

"I don't know why you think I'm a gearhead."

"Because you say things like 'one foot in front of the other.' "

"Oh," he said, dashing his cigarette on the asphalt. "I thought I was being poetic."

"Everybody thinks that about themselves."

"You guys need help schlepping stuff? If you make it to the Whisky show, Toby will probably let me use one of the vans. I can be your driver."

"Why would he do that?"

He grinned. "I'm dependable."

"Thanks, Jeff," I said. "I hadn't thought about it. That would be good."

"Just keep making the music, Street. That's your new job."

He walked off, and I sat staring up at the moon, which had jumped out of nowhere.

Sometimes I pretended the moon cared about me.

Just like I pretended my father did.

Ed the Guitar Guy

The next night I was sitting in my room dashing through my homework so I could get back to working on my songs when my mother tapped on my door. I looked at my watch and was surprised she was still home because this was certainly the having-pots-of-tea-with-Louise-at-the-Fig-Tree hour. My stomach knotted up because I knew she wanted to have one of those talks.

I hadn't really told her about the band. How could she know? I wasn't ready to talk yet. "Mom, I've got an AP history test next week."

"This won't take long."

The door opened and she walked in with a tall, skinny guy her age who had dark blond hair to his shoulders, wide blue eyes, suntan wrinkles, six earrings and a nose stud. He wore Levi's and a long-sleeved shirt untucked and stood with his hands on his hips smiling at me.

"This is Ed," she said. "Ed, this is Blanche."

"Hi, Blanche. Nice name."

I was too stunned to say anything.

My mother didn't generally bring men home. I knew she dated them occasionally, but she was very particular about who she let into the house. In all the time my father had been gone I'd met two guys. One was Lance the corporate attorney who wore squeaky loafers and short-sleeved button-down shirts and said "sweet" a lot.

Lance lasted exactly one month.

Next came Timothy and he lasted almost six months because he was broody and depressed and had a novel that no one would publish. She'd never admit it but I think my mom gave him some money. For some reason, he got a grant to continue his novel-in-progress and he went off to a writers' colony in New York and that was that. I wasn't sure who dumped whom but the whole scenario was a little too much like the one with my father.

Ed didn't look like either one of those extremes. He was something in the middle.

Anyway, back to my name.

My mother couldn't resist filling him in on the history:

"She's not named after Blanche DuBois, which is what everyone thinks. She's named after Blanchefleur . . ."

"Oh," he said, "from Tristan and Isolde."

I wish you could have seen the look on my mother's face. It made me very nervous.

"Yes," she half whispered.

"It's a pretty well-known legend," I said to calm her down.

"Tristan's mother, Blanchefleur. Which of course means 'white flower' in French," my mother said.

"Sure, sure," Ed said. He was looking around my room like an idiot savant, like one of those people who'd be able to re-create an exact replica later. Still letting his eyes surf across my walls, he said to my mother, "Diane, you're a true romantic."

"Well, I wasn't the only one. Her father loved that story, too. We saw the play together at some artsy playhouse in Hollywood. That's how it started."

"You guys probably want to have a longer discussion about this somewhere. Nice to meet you, Ed."

"Oh, honey, Ed is here for a reason. He opened up a guitar store down the street from Biscuit." Biscuit, if you'll recall, was the curiously named clothing store that Mom and Louise ran together. They named it that because it was Louise's cat's name. You could not come up with a worse marketing strategy if you tried, but somehow it was working.

Biscuit was for women who were tired of wearing clothes. Long flowy skirts and silk pants with elastic waists and scarves and hats to disguise the fact that you were really wearing pajamas. Neither my mother nor Louise dressed like that. Mom still had some rock-and-roll girlfriend in her and Louise wore anything tight to show off the body that she constantly starved and the boobs that had suddenly appeared last Christmas.

People in the program were not hard on themselves about anything other than substance abuse. They felt that was the only test they needed to pass, so that's why Louise gave herself permission to be anorexic and my mother didn't wear makeup and dressed too young and ate a lot of sugar.

"Really," I said. "What kind of guitar shop?"

"Small," he said.

"What kind of guitars do you have?" I asked.

"Little bit of everything."

"Do you play?"

"Yeah, sure."

"He went to Berklee," my mother explained. "It's a music college."

"I was in some bands when I was young but the weird thing is, I always liked the tools more than the trade, you know, so eventually I just started selling guitars and now I have my own shop."

He said all this as if he were answering some question he was always asked, like from the press, so he was prepared.

"What's it called?" I asked.

"Ed's Guitars," Ed said.

"Well, that's very precise."

I could see my mother getting nervous about my tone so she started talking fast: "I asked Ed if he'd take a look at your guitar. You know, it has that crack in the top."

"You mean Dad's guitar?"

"Yes," she said. "You know what I mean."

"I like the crack," I said.

"Well, let me just take a look," Ed said.

I pulled the guitar out from under my bed and he studied it. He twirled it around in his big hands, looked inside the sound hole, looked at the back of the neck, and held it up to eye level, never losing his grin. What was he grinning at? What was just randomly and consistently pleasing to him?

"My dad was kind of famous," I said.

"I know who he is. The crack's not too bad."

"Ed and I have talked about that," my mother said, narrowing her eyes at me.

"I'd leave it alone unless it bugs you," he said.

"What do you mean?"

"The crack. I wouldn't bother trying to do anything with it. Replacing the top would change the guitar. I don't think you want to do that."

"No, I don't."

"I could give it a setup," he said. "Get rid of the buzz on the low E. I'd do it for free, no problem."

"Maybe," I said. I didn't want to admit the low E string had a buzz but it did.

They stood there for a long uncomfortable minute and then it was Ed who said to my mother, "Let's go to the Urth Café and get a coffee or something. Blanche looks busy."

"Yeah, okay."

"You in the program, Ed?"

"What?"

"AA. That how you guys met?"

"No, we met at my store. Your mom came by to check it out."

"Awesome."

Mom touched his arm and said, "Ed, go on and I'll meet you at Urth."

"You sure?"

"Yes," she said, looking at me.

"Nice to meet you," he said and went out.

"What's that accent of his? He sounds like the movie *Fargo*."

"He's from the Midwest. Blanche, really, did I raise you to be rude or is this something you picked up on your own?"

"I thought brutal honesty was the policy of the program."

"You're not in the program. You're a teenager who's expected to be courteous to people in our house."

"He's a guitar salesman. Ed the Guitar Guy."

"What's your point?"

"It's a little far to fall, Mom. Rock star to guitar salesman."

She stared hard at me and I wasn't at all sure what she was going to do because I couldn't remember ever having talked to her that way. I wasn't sure why I was doing it now.

"Your father," she said, "is not here. You may have noticed."

"So that's Ed's big selling point? He's here?"

She ran her fingers through her hair and took a breath and stared at the wall. I could imagine she was following some AA rhyming rule like "When in doubt, leave it out."

She said, "Ed and I are going to Urth. I want you to apologize the next time you see him."

"Fine," I said. I didn't want to talk about it anymore because something on my computer screen had caught my eye.

His name had jumped up in my in-box.

She went out and I waited until I heard the front door close and then I clicked on my dad's screen name: Ineffable1. The title box said "Keep Me Informed."

I read the e-mail over and over:

Hello Lovely One. Interesting news about the band. If I were a responsible father I'd say, don't do it. But you're going to follow your own path. If music is calling you, resistance is futile. Just know that it will lead you places you never counted on going. But you will go wherever you are going to go. Just don't make music your partner. It is unreliable and will betray you at every turn. Still, you can't help loving it if you do.

My advice about playing at the Whisky or anywhere is to be nice to the sound guy. Also, when playing live, think about something to make your sound dynamic. I recommend a tempo change. Right in the middle. When the timing of the music suddenly changes, and everybody goes with it, it looks like faith. But it's really practice.

I read the e-mail over and over until I memorized it.

Then I got out his cracked guitar and started putting some chords together for a song I would later call "Looks Like Faith."

The next day I told the band about Ed the Guitar Guy. I told them about "Keep Me Informed." I found I was telling them everything. I had to because everything that happened to me now had a place to land. Every funny story, strange character or strong emotion worked its way toward a song that I had a reason to write.

It was a little uncomfortable, letting people into my life that way. I hadn't told anyone that I still talked to my father because I was afraid he'd stop contacting me. I kept my promise about not telling anyone where he was, but for a long time, I never breathed a word about even knowing he was alive.

The great thing about Gigi and Viv and Ella was that other than a rudimentary understanding of their instruments, they didn't know the first thing about music so they didn't care about my father. Other than he was my father.

Viv said it was strange, she couldn't imagine her father the physicist doing anything cool. He was one step away from taping his glasses together. Her mother had to lay his clothes out for him because his head was always so preoccupied he couldn't bother to tell what matched.

Ella said her father owned a trucking company and all he did was work and when he came home from work he drank beer. Her mother kept herself busy scrapbooking and driving her five brothers around. Ella was the youngest and a mistake. Her mother was so worn out by then that she didn't have the energy to figure out how to raise a daughter differently so Ella was raised as a son and that was why she was the way she was.

"I'm not gay, though," she said. "Not that there's anything wrong with being gay but everyone thinks I am and I'm not."

"Grow your hair," Gigi suggested.

"I wouldn't know what to do with it."

"I'll show you. I'm good at it. We'll do a makeover."

"You'd have to come over every day. It's easier like this."

I told her not to change it; the look was good for the band and besides, she'd find someone who liked her because she was different. I had some success with that.

"You mean like Jeff?" she asked.

"Jeff's a friend."

"You don't like him?"

"He's a geek and he works in a pizza shop."

"You're holding out for the rock star?" Viv asked.

"Who isn't?"

They both said they weren't but I thought they were lying.

I complained some more about Ed the Guitar Guy and how my mother was settling for him. And that's how we started talking about guitar stores. Viv remembered that Guitar Center was just right down the street from school and suggested we go there.

"I can't stand it there," Gigi said. "My father likes to go in there and look around. It's loud and there are all these pimply adolescent boys playing bad guitar and the salespeople are jerks and they all look like rejects from some Depeche Mode tribute band."

"Sounds great," Ella said. "Let's go during lunch."

So we did.

I didn't think it was my imagination that we all moved a little differently walking down the street to Guitar Center. I could have sworn we were swaggering. Before we were just Laurel Hall kids and we were aware of people looking at us as if something were fundamentally wrong with us because we went to such a joke of a school. (People were probably never thinking that; we were thinking that.) But now we moved like a rock band.

We went into Guitar Center and it was exactly the way Gigi described. We walked around all the guitars and touched them and played them. We went through the keyboards and banged on them, and Viv sang into one of the mikes and then we went to the drums and Ella played a little, which caused all the guys to look at us, even the salesmen who'd been ignoring us because, since we were girls, they thought we weren't going to buy anything. But once Ella played, people paid attention and she felt it and blushed.

I left that scene because it was a good opportunity to slip away and try out a pink Telecaster I had my eye on. I had never imagined myself playing an electric guitar but because this one was pink I felt I was allowed to touch it. It was already plugged in so I picked it up and strummed it and it sounded great, like a chime with some muscle to it, and everything I did on it sounded like a legitimate noise, not like an accident the way the acoustic guitar sometimes sounded. A guy with long hair and a nose ring came over and asked if he could answer any questions and I couldn't think of any except "How much is it?" And he said it was whatever it was and I didn't really listen because I knew it wasn't forty-seven dollars which was how much money I had in my checking account after I'd paid for books and uniforms. I thanked him and he walked away but said over his shoulder, "It looks good on you."

I thought about being offended because he should have

said something about my playing, which was more than most girls knew. Then I thought it wasn't such a bad thing to say a guitar looked good on a person and I was still thinking about that when the others returned and said we should get back to school.

If we had left a second earlier. If Ella hadn't played the drums, if I hadn't picked up the Telecaster, if we hadn't gone there at all but used the time instead to study as we usually did. That's the kind of bargaining you do when you look back at a twist of fate, lying in the path like something that accidentally flew out the window. We were walking down Sunset Boulevard three blocks from where we'd turn to go safely back to LaHa when I think it was Gigi who said, "Hey, we've never been in here, either. Let's go in."

It was your typical New Agey incense store with crystals and Buddhas and selections of tea. It was called Sanctuary Tide, which seemed like two words that didn't belong together, but it conjured images of all your dreams coming true and stuff so we went in.

There were wind chimes and candles and everything smelled like church and there was some distant flute playing. Buddhas were everywhere, side by side with African masks and some Shiva the destroyers, and that Hindu elephant god with extra arms. I felt nervous. My mother was always dragging me into stores like that when I was little, on her search for whatever was going to save her, and she changed religions or spiritual disciplines the way most people changed their hairstyles.

This was in the beginning of the program when she felt she needed some kind of concrete image of God in order to surrender to Him. She went through every imaginable icon on her altar before giving up and deciding He was the Energy that picked up where hers ran out. He was, she said, doing all the things we only thought we were doing. She said things like "It's not your will that makes everything work, Blanche. It just isn't."

But in Sanctuary Tide, the other girls were poking around and laughing and smelling things while the woman behind the counter with dreadlocks and nineteen piercings and tattoos on her neck glared at them in a way that wasn't very bodhisattva. I was ready to leave.

"Come on, you guys," I said.

They didn't hear me. They were intrigued with something over in the corner.

I could feel the eyes of Dreds bearing down on us.

"Guys, we're going to be late," I insisted.

The others were lifting the top off an ornate wooden and brass canister. It had wire mesh at the top with a little piggy-bank type slit and you could look through and see little pieces of paper piling up at the bottom.

"What is it?" I asked.

"Fancy trash can, I guess," Gigi said.

It had some kind of hieroglyphic writing on it, which meant it was especially holy. God spoke Chinese or Egyptian or Latin, never English.

From across the room, Dreds said, "It's a prayer box."

"What's that?" Viv asked.

"It's a thing you put prayers in, genius," Ella said.

"Why would you put prayers in something?" Gigi asked.

By now Dreds had flip-flopped her way over to us.

"It's my favorite thing in the store," she said in a serious tone. She reeked of clove cigarettes and she had Chinese symbols tattooed across both hands to match the ones on her neck. "What you do is you offer your most sacred prayer and the box contains it for you."

"Why would you want a prayer to be contained?" Ella asked. "Wouldn't you want it to go to heaven?"

"Why would you need to write it down?" said Gigi. "God can't hear?"

"Writing something down impresses the unconscious," Dreds said a little impatiently, "and the unconscious communicates directly with Spirit. So it's a faster process."

"So it's like the FedEx of praying," Viv said.

I laughed. "Good one. You are coming along, grasshopper. You're getting the hang of relentless sarcasm."

"Mocking the Spirit doesn't make it less real," said Dreds in a serious tone.

"A prayer box doesn't make it more real," Viv said with a degree of haughtiness. "My father's a physicist and my mother's a biologist and they say there's no empirical evidence of anything but a random and indifferent universe." (She said this like it was something she memorized because she didn't understand what it meant but it carried a lot of weight at her house. The way, ironically, some people memorize prayers.)

"Here's what you do," Dreds said, deciding that Viv wasn't worth arguing with. "You take a piece of paper, you write your prayer on it, you put it in the prayer box. You don't think about the prayer again. If you think about it again, it takes the power away from it because it exhibits a lack of faith. The universe, see, is very literal and if you offer something to it, it will provide what you want but it can't connect as powerfully if you keep doubting it. It interferes with the energetic communion."

"Well, we wouldn't want to do that," Ella said.

"It's the way you don't talk about a wish that you make." Dreds powered on. "Everything leaks energy when you transfer it or translate it."

"Does it cost anything to give it a shot?" Gigi asked.

"No."

"Then I'm game."

Gigi took the pad of paper and pencil that were sitting by the prayer box. She scribbled on a piece of the paper and dropped it in the canister.

"Do I have to chant or anything now?" she asked Dreds.

"No."

"Awesome."

To my surprise, Ella followed suit and dropped in a prayer. Viv scoffed and then said she was going to do it just to prove it didn't work. That left me as the holdout and I had to go for it because I didn't feel we had time for an argument. I scribbled something quickly and dropped it in and then, at last, we could leave.

Dreds was happy to see us go. We ran back to school and we missed the second bell and we all got demerit slips.

The No-Talent Show

THE FIRST THING THAT WENT WRONG: THE IDEA CAUGHT ON.

Every day when I walked past the talent roster, I saw another new act, until there were almost twenty acts signed up. This up from four when the roster first appeared.

Some of the Chelseas from choir decided they would sing an a cappella song, and one of the computer Joshes revealed that he could play the accordion. There were a flute player and a stand-up comedian, three jugglers, one combo Hula Hoop routine/magic act, and some pet tricks.

"No competition," Gigi said. "We're going to sweep."

I wasn't so sure anymore. Especially when I witnessed the second thing that went wrong. We were setting up inside the Art Deco auditorium—it had been a supper club when the school was a hotel, so it had a round stage and tapestry chairs and booths along the walls. I was looking around to see how the tiles and the carpet were going to affect the acoustics when I saw my mother walking in. That was bad enough but she had brought Ed the Guitar Guy. I couldn't remember how to breathe.

Viv saw my expression. "Dude, is that your mother?"

"Yes."

"Oh, my God, why did you invite your mom?" Gigi asked. "Nobody lets parents in on this stuff."

"I didn't."

"How'd she find out?"

"I don't know."

Ed the Guitar Guy saw my approach before my mother did and I had to give him credit, he read my body language correctly. His smile vanished and he started tapping my mother on the arm. Mom looked at me and she didn't bat an eye at my demeanor.

"What do you think you're doing?" I asked.

"I wanted to see."

"This is not for you."

She just smiled.

"Mom, seriously, don't you realize you're embarrassing me?"

"I'm always embarrassing you. But I wanted to see you play."

"How did you even find out?"

"The school sends me e-mails, Blanche. I do know how to read e-mails."

"I think it's my fault," Ed the Guitar Guy said. "I suggested coming. Your mom said you'd hate it."

"Stop being noble, Ed," my mother said. "It was

completely my idea and I asked him to come with me. I intended to sneak in the back and you'd never know I was here. I guess we were early."

"I don't care whose idea it was because I have a brand-new idea. You go home now."

"You can't blame your mom for wanting to see this," said Ed the Guitar Guy. "She's proud of you. She is being quite nice especially since you never told her."

I looked at him. "I'm sorry. Have we barely met?"

Mr. Carmichael, who was running the whole show, chose that moment to come over and say hello so I had to introduce them and then he showed them where the best place to sit was so that they could see and hear perfectly.

At that point, I had lost the battle.

"So at least sit in the back where I can't see you?" I asked.

"Well, we're here now and I wouldn't want to hurt your teacher's feelings," Mom said. She smiled at me.

When I made my way back over to the Fringers they had all the equipment set up and were pretending like they hadn't been staring.

"Who's the guy?" Viv asked.

"Ed the Guitar Guy. Just act like it's not happening."

I could feel tears pushing their way up and I didn't want anyone to see it. I couldn't admit to them what was really bothering me. Playing in front of a bunch of kids who went to the worst private school in L.A. wasn't all that intimidating. But the woman who was married to Duncan Kelly and her new boyfriend who'd gone to Berklee was something I wasn't ready for. Plus I'd been so sure we were going to win and now, with all the new competition piling up, and my confidence shaken, I wasn't sure we could even place. What if we lost to jugglers or someone in a Hula Hoop? How would one walk away from that, head held high?

Suddenly I thought about putting one foot in front of the other. Jeff told me that. Seeing his face only made things worse. At least it was only in my imagination, unlike other faces I knew. My stomach was hurting and I didn't think I could remember how to make a G chord and I wished with everything in my body that I hadn't started this. I missed my life of a recluse and my music column and being someone who had opinions instead of trying to take action.

But it was too late for any of that.

I stood backstage with the Fringers and watched all the acts. The Chelseas were pretty good and they had thought about wearing matching outfits. We were just wearing our uniforms—it hadn't occurred to me that we could break dress code for this. One juggler was good and the Hula Hoop magic act wasn't terrible and the comedian got three big laughs.

When we took the stage, I could see all the faces. I thought they would blur and run together but they didn't. I could see eyes and expressions and body language. People were waiting.

But mostly I saw my mother and Ed the Guitar Guy. They were actually trying to hunker down in their seats but they might as well have been standing right in front of me.

My guitar buzzed when I first turned on the amp but I

quickly adjusted, and as I heard Ella count us in and I was staring at the expectant faces, this idea raced through my brain:

I'm up here and you're not. I'm willing.

Yep, my dad's idea. The difference between us and them was willingness.

No one could blame me for being willing. I concentrated.

The music was playing and I remembered all the chords and I was able to do some tricks I didn't even think I knew. The applause and the whooping started before we even got to the bridge and Viv was singing as if her whole life depended on it. My eyes roamed around the room and I saw Dr. Bonny, in a purple suit, chomping Altoids and smiling. Next to her, Dr. Morleymower was openmouthed, and next to him Mr. Carmichael couldn't resist bobbing his head.

It was over before I wanted it to be. We wrapped it up and I messed up this fancy ending I had learned but it didn't matter because people were on their feet and the Fringers were really born.

Dr. Bonny gave us the trophy, handing it to Viv, who promptly handed it over to me, and it seemed like the applause went on for half a day.

I saw my mother and Ed the Guitar Guy beaming and suddenly their presence didn't bug me so much.

I imagined my father watching and smiling.

I was convinced that wherever he was he could feel it happening.

And suddenly, for the first time, I was starting to understand who he was and what he became and why he wanted to be that guy.

When we were leaving the auditorium—stopping every two seconds, it seemed, to accept congratulations and even to sign some autographs—Gigi leaned over to me and said, "It's really weird."

"What?"

"That's what I put in the prayer box. That we would win the talent show."

"Gigi, odds were great that we were going to win the talent show. Us or the Hula Hoop act."

"I know, it's just a little weird."

"It's not even a little weird. It's common sense. We earned it."

"I'm just saying."

"Hang in there," I said. "Don't wig. We have a long road ahead. And besides, we have Ella to supply all our needs for weird."

The Whisky A Go Go

Here are the people who've played there since it was established in 1964: the Byrds, Alice Cooper, Buffalo Springfield, Love, the Doors, Jimi Hendrix, Sam and Dave, the Turtles, the Kinks, the Who, Cream, Led Zeppelin, Roxy Music, Oasis, X, Mötley Crüe, Van Halen, Van Morrison, the Ramones, the Misfits, Blondie, Talking Heads, Elvis Costello.

And Duncan Kelly.

My parents used to tell stories about it when I was little. I didn't pay much attention because of two things. I didn't know he was going to leave and I didn't know I was going to be a musician myself. The main story I remembered was that it was supposed to be haunted. I remembered being at the table when my father was telling stories about people who had experienced sightings and my mom said, "Duncan, they're musicians, they're haunted wherever they go." And they laughed. I wasn't old enough to know what that meant. But I knew they had some kind of secret language. It was the moment I realized my parents had a life that predated me. It was a thought that cheered me and that I conjured whenever I got worried about them. Whenever they fought. When my father stayed in the studios for days. When he didn't have time for us. When he was cranky. When he was drinking. When she was drinking about his drinking. It drove my mother crazy, his moodiness and his creative attacks, but I always wondered why it surprised her. Didn't she know he was a musician? Didn't she know there was a price to pay for that?

I knew that I blamed my mother for giving up on him. I knew that I thought if she'd only been more patient, smarter, more creative herself, he would have stuck around. I also knew how completely wrong and unfair that was. I had made a little headway into changing my mind and then Ed the Guitar Guy. What's a girl supposed to do?

If Ed, now known to me as ETG, wasn't evidence of a woman underachieving, honoring her lowest self, I didn't know what was.

I mean, this guy gave up on being a musician and settled for just selling stuff to other musicians. He must have wanted to do something great at one time. Where did that go? He had played in some L.A. bands (so he said, I had not heard of them), had toured the country and Europe once, had had some songs published and even recorded by other artists. And then one day, he chucked it all and opened a guitar store. What the hell was that?

Ed only laughed when I asked him. (I asked him more politely.)

Sometimes he'd say the thing about liking the tool more than the trade. This was clearly his stock answer he'd come up with for any time he was challenged on it, like Viv's answer to God. Sometimes he'd say, "I didn't like all the drama. You gotta like the drama a little bit." Sometimes he'd say, "I saw too many friends die from it." The last one he'd pull out when I got particularly belligerent.

Mom seemed to think he was the greatest. She laughed at his lame jokes. She hung on his every word. She didn't have to tell me any of that. I saw the way she looked at him.

It wasn't just that she was giving up on my dad ever coming back. It was that now I knew she made a lie out of ever wanting him or being with him. How could that woman want Duncan Kelly one minute, Ed the Guitar Guy the next? It made no sense.

Unless she had given up on anything great or magical in life.

When Thanksgiving came around, instead of ignoring it and taking me to In-N-Out and a movie the way she usually did—which might sound depressing but it was our thing and it was fun—she made the traditional turkey-and-stuffing dinner and had ETG over and they both put on dressy clothes. He wore a sports jacket and a turtleneck and loafers. She put on a tight black dress and heels. I sat there in my jeans and Clash T-shirt and shook my head, watching them putter around the kitchen and make noises of satisfaction over the food.

"We never do this, you know," I told Ed. "We usually ignore Thanksgiving."

"Me too," he said. "But it's nice to have someone to celebrate it with."

"We had each other. Before you."

"Yeah, I know, I'm horning in."

"We could have all gone to a movie. I'm not saying you're not welcome. I'm just saying it's not clear why we had to change our whole tradition."

My mother smiled at me, but it was that oh-brother-what-have-I-created smile.

She said, "We can still go to a movie later. Or you can go to one by yourself after our meal. The bus goes all over town."

"Kicked out. Awesome."

"You are being a pill," she said. "Is that part of being in a rock band?"

"No, it's part of being—"

I almost said *your daughter* but I knew that one would get me grounded.

I didn't really feel that way but I felt like I felt that way.

I didn't understand the complicated mess that was me.

Later, after dinner, ETG explained it to me.

Mom was washing dishes and I was fooling with my guitar and staring at a football game in the living room and he sat down next to me.

"Football fan?" he asked.

"No. Nor a talking-about-it fan."

He sighed and said, "Well, we're going to talk about it."

I was surprised, and I had to admit, a little pleased to see a bit of spine on him.

"Nervous about the Whisky show?" he asked.

"No. Why do you say that?"

"Because when I had shows coming up, I used to get nervous, but I didn't know how to be nervous so I just got mean."

"When did you have shows?" I asked him.

"I told you. I used to play live a lot. I had a bit of a following."

"You don't have to explain," I said.

"I'm just saying, everybody gets nervous before a show."

"I don't think that accounts for my disposition."

"Well, maybe it's Coachella."

Now I was really staring at him. The last thing I needed was some guitar salesman reading my thoughts and seeing into my soul.

But first.

A short tutorial on Coachella. Many of you know it is a very famous outdoor music festival outside Palm Desert, in Coachella Valley, just two hours out of town. People come from all over the world to see it. Why would I even dream about playing there? Because the winner of the Whisky High School Band night automatically qualified for the latest event, which was the Unsigned Competition.

"Coachella? I don't know what you're talking about," I said.

He smiled. "Well, they even let old guys and guitar salesmen use the Internet, so I noticed on the Whisky Web site that the winners of the High School Band Night get to go there and I was thinking, if I were playing at High School Band Night, I'd be hoping like crazy that I would win so I could go to Coachella."

"Beautiful linear thought process, Ed."

"I'm proud of it."

"Does my mom know?"

"Hasn't said anything. Would she mind?"

"I think so. Being in the talent show is one thing because it's just school. But the Whisky is making her a little uncomfortable because it looks like I want to be a musician. You can imagine how she'd feel about Coachella."

"Do you want to be a musician?" he asked.

"Not really."

"Do you write songs?"

"No," I lied. "Not on purpose. I'm just doing this for my résumé. You know, the college thing."

"Okay," he said.

"The last thing I consider myself is an artist."

He laughed. "Because that's such a terrible thing to be?"

"Ask my mother."

"This isn't about her or your father. It's about you."

"No, Ed, I don't want to be an artist. It isn't about wanting. I'm not one."

"If you feel compelled to write songs, you might be an artist."

I thought about the contraband under my mattress. I was damned if I'd let him into that world.

"I'm a student. And a critic. I'm going to get into a good

college. If I play music, that's the only reason why. Because it will look good on my application. It's research for my future."

"Okay," he said.

"Means to an end and all that."

"Okay," he said again.

"Okay," I responded.

He was quiet for a minute. Then he said, "She got burned by him and she's not over it. And she's not wrong that it's sometimes hard to live with an artist. Including yourself if you're the artist. You have to work hard to stay grounded and not lose yourself. But between you and me, you have to be what you are. If you have a calling, you can't fight it."

"Let's say I have a calling. Who or what is doing the calling?"

"That's a good question."

"Yet people talk about callings all the time like it's a real thing."

"I guess it's something supernatural. Like God."

"Don't worry. God doesn't call me. I'm not an artist. And it's my life."

"Well, hell, she knows that. But your mom is just trying to give you some guidance. She knows you don't have to listen to it."

I was quiet.

He said, "She's just taking it one day at a time."

"Yeah, I understand about the program."

"Well, I'm not talking about that. I'm just talking about life."

"She's my mother," I said. "You don't have to tell me about her."

"You're right about that."

Still I couldn't leave the room.

He said, "Anytime you decide to go for something, it's going to upset somebody."

"Is that why you gave up? Because it was upsetting people?"

He laughed. "No. Because it stopped upsetting people. That's when you know you're not an artist. You're something else."

"Like what? A guitar salesman?"

"Sure," he said. "An artist needs his tools. I'm the guy who helps him find it. Or her."

His smile was annoyingly peaceful. Like he really had found his calling.

More Madrigals

Every year the Madrigals performed a lame holiday concert and this year was no exception. The only exception was that I was part of it and I had to put on the lame red sweater over our usual uniforms, which were plaid skirts and polos. We looked like Christmas pillows. We sang the James Taylor song that all the Chelseas had complained about and we sang some holiday-neutral songs to keep all the PC folks happy and we sang some Christmas songs that could get away with being Christmas songs because they were considered classical.

Gigi and Ella came to show support for me and Viv. Their support really took the form of sneering and making faces from the audience.

Viv's parents, the famous scientists, came, and sat front

row because they actually approved of her being in Madrigals. They were a little more concerned about the Fringers because we seemed to be goofing off. But winning the talent show had turned them around a little and now they were beginning to get the point.

Dr. and Dr. Wyler sat in the front row, with straight posture but rumpled clothes, and watched all the activity as if they found it all so fascinating, the way that the humans behaved. My mom and Ed the Guitar Guy sat next to them and as they leaned across each other and whispered, I wondered what in the world they had to discuss.

Right before the lights went out, I saw a guy in the back of the room who I knew for a fact wasn't one of the Joshes at LaHa. He was wearing something with a complicated print and his hair was purposely haywire and dyed. I barely got a look at him before the ambience turned violet and we were singing "Fire and Rain."

People clapped and went nuts when it was over and acted like we'd reinvented the whole choir-singing wheel, and all the Chelseas ate it up. I had a polite conversation with Viv's parents. Dr. Mr. Wyler said, "Remarkable, girls, remarkable. This is what happens when ingenuity and creativity converge."

Mom said, "Have you thought about what you're wearing at the Whisky show?"

I said, "You're looking at it, minus the sweaters."

"Oh," Dr. Mrs. Wyler said. "Oh, is that a good idea? It's like you're representing the school."

"And it's not very rock and roll," Dr. Mr. Wyler said,

in the way that only people who never say "rock and roll" can.

"That's Blanche's idea," Viv said. "She thinks LaHa is a fringe school, so that makes us the Fringers. See?"

"I like it," Ed the Guitar Guy said, smiling his Midwestern smile.

I'd had enough of all this family unity so I made my excuses and went outside to find Ella and Gigi. Viv trailed behind me, with the doctors saying, "Don't linger, Vivien, the hour progresses."

They were standing in a two-person huddle looking at something and whispering. Viv and I walked up, and before I could say anything Gigi was hissing, "Don't speak. Don't look around. Just freeze."

This didn't sound like a reasonable plan to me so I looked over my shoulder and said, "What?"

Gigi gasped and Ella said, "Typical. I told you not to say that."

"What am I looking at?"

"Redmond Dwayne," Gigi hissed again.

"Who is that? Why are you hissing?"

"He's in the Clauses," she said.

By now I had found him in the after-Madrigals crowd, the guy with the wild print and rebellious hair. He was standing apart from everyone and had his arms crossed and seemed to be looking right at us.

"What are the Clauses?"

Ella said, "It's a band. They used to be the Viruses. They go to Brentwood."

"They're the biggest L.A. band," Gigi said.

"Bigger than Maroon 5?"

"She means unsigned band. You know what she means," Ella said.

"I heard they already have an agent," Viv said.

I looked at them, shocked. "You guys thought Celine Dion was music when I met you."

"Okay, we've been doing our research," Gigi said. "I mean, we're part of the band scene now."

"Oh, my God, he's coming over," Viv said, turning her back toward him.

"What does he want?" Gigi asked, grabbing my arm.

"You're kidding, right? Asking me that."

"Hey," came this deep voice, nothing like the Joshes' voices. This one had changed. He sounded like a man. Or he was making himself sound like that, anyway.

None of us said anything.

"Who's Viv?" he asked.

"Me," Viv said in a near-whisper.

"You've got that band, the Fringers."

"It's Blanche's band, really," she said.

He looked at me briefly.

"It's all our band," I said.

"She writes the songs," Viv said. "I just sing them."

He nodded, dividing his gaze between the two of us. Then he looked at Gigi and Ella. They introduced themselves this way: "Bass." "Drums."

"Nice to meet you, bass and drums," he said. Turning to me, he raised an eyebrow and said, "Guitar?"

"Yes."

"You're playing at the Whisky. High School Band Night."

"Right," I said.

"Us too. I saw you on the roster."

"Oh, so you don't have . . . you're not signed . . ."

"We don't have a major," he said. "I mean, we're about to. But we still qualify. For this and Coachella."

"What's at Coachella?" Viv asked.

I looked at my feet and Redmond Dwayne explained the whole thing to the girls. When I looked back up they were staring at me.

"Is that what you've got in mind?" Gigi whispered. "And you're keeping it from us?"

"I'm mainly keeping it from my mom."

"Oh, my God," Viv said. "Playing at Coachella."

"I didn't even know if you guys knew what it was," I said.

Ella said, "That's the coolest thing ever."

"Don't anybody get excited," I said. "We still have to win at the Whisky."

"Yeah," Redmond said. "You still have to do that."

He smiled at us, letting that look flit across each of us just long enough to give each of us hope, and then he moved away.

"Did you see his eyes?" Gigi said.

"Did you see his nose stud?" Viv said.

I didn't see anything but competition.

Competition

I ADMIT I EXPECTED TO SEE PICTURES OF MY FATHER ON THE wall in the Whisky when we went in. My mother had warned me about that. But I wasn't prepared for how it made me feel. While the rest of the band was tuning up, I found myself staring at my father's face, ten years younger than I even remembered. He was wearing black leather, a studded belt, bed hair, a three-day beard, and black sunglasses, and holding a guitar in one hand and a cigarette in the other. He was tall and skinny and his posture was apologetic, though I suspected that was just his thing. His act. I didn't remember him being apologetic about anything.

My mother stood over my shoulder and said, "That was his *Easy Rider* year. He only had that look for the first record. Then he started thermal T-shirts and really short hair. He kept changing his look so nobody could define him."

I smiled. I had gotten one of those pearls of advice from him before. "Don't have a style and that includes not having a style," I said without thinking.

Mom looked at me. "What?"

"Oh, it's something he said to me in an e-mail."

A flicker of surprise passed over her face. "You still talk to him?"

"Sure. E-mail." I heard her silence. "Why, don't you?"

"No."

It didn't occur to me that they didn't talk to each other. I just assumed they had the same kind of sporadic contact that he and I did.

Ed the Guitar Guy seemed to anticipate her shift in mood and knew what to do with it.

"Better go tune up," he said. "Your mom and I'll wait outside. Don't want to make you nervous."

"I can't get any more nervous," I said, though it wasn't true. Realizing I'd suddenly upset my mother was adding to the stress. It was one thing to upset her when I was trying to. But I had just stepped into this. Very bad timing.

Ed put his arm around her and ushered her outside.

I was thinking about following. Then I turned and saw Redmond Dwayne staring at me. Which didn't make me relax but certainly took my mind off my mother.

He said, "That's your dad."

"No, that's my mom's friend."

"I mean in the picture. Duncan Kelly."

"Yeah."

"You look a little like him."

I smiled. I couldn't see it but I was flattered that he did.

"I love his stuff," he said.

"Really?" Mostly kids my age had no idea who he was.

He said, "Your dad and Paul Westerberg are my favorites. You know, the Replacements."

"He liked them, too. I think maybe he knew Paul Westerberg. My mom says he did."

"Cool," Redmond Dwayne said. He was wearing his sunglasses inside, which is rarely a good thing, but somehow he was making it work.

"You guys gonna change or is that what you're wearing?" he asked. We'd both been thinking about fashion at the same time.

"No, the school uniforms are our look. Because LaHa is a fringe school. We're not like the others."

I made a sweeping gesture toward all the Brentwood, Harvard Westlake, Marlborough and Crossroads kids piling in with their expensive amps and instruments. To a person, they were all being guided by their parents, who were in rich-people-go-casual clothes. I didn't envy these kids because their parents were way too involved in what was going on, like they were the ones who were getting up onstage. They knew that agents and managers might be in the crowd and they were invested in their kids getting famous. So they could be famous for being their parents.

I appreciated my mother and her resistance to it all. I appreciated her being outside and upset. Even though I had upset her. It just felt more genuine. An artist was supposed to have a little turmoil.

Not that I was an artist.

"Well, I guess it's no wonder, then," Redmond said. "Considering who your dad is."

"No wonder what?"

He hesitated. "You're so talented. You know."

"You haven't seen us play."

"I've heard the rumors," he said.

"No, you meant that it's no wonder we made it this far. Because of who my dad is. Believe me, nobody knows who my dad is."

"I wasn't talking about nepotism," he said.

"Sure you were."

"Look, don't get so defensive. We can have it out on-stage. That's where we'll figure out who's what."

I wanted to kick him. I also wanted to kiss him. Which was strange.

"Hey, Street, where do you want this?"

I turned to see Jeff lugging my amp in. I'd forgotten about him. I'd ridden in the van with him on the way over and already I'd forgotten him. This was how rock and roll worked. This was what my mom was talking about. It made you forget yourself and where you came from and who helped you get there.

"Oh, just over by the stage. Thanks, Jeff."

"Your boyfriend?" Redmond asked.

"Friend. Volunteer roadie."

" 'Street'? What's that?"

"He calls me that."

He waited.

"Blanche. *Streetcar Named Desire.* Though I'm not really named for that . . ."

He smiled, losing interest. "Good luck, Street."

"Yeah, you too," I said, and watched him saunter across the floor toward the Clauses, all weaker impersonations of him.

I won't make you sit through the whole lineup of bands the way I had to. Here are the highlights. Redmond Dwayne's band the Clauses opened and they were the best. They did this high-energy set full of angst-ridden songs and Redmond played really loud Telecaster through a crunchy amp and sang like, no surprise, Paul Westerberg. After them, a lot of the bands were nothing special. The Patients, a band from Crossroads, were all dressed in hospital gowns, and at the end of the set they all pantomimed fainting and were carried off the stage on stretchers. Their songs sounded like bad Beatles. The Zoo were all dressed like exotic animals. You see where this is going. There was one really good band from Santa Monica High, just synthesizers and a girl who could sing okay, but nothing like Viv. There was only one other all-girl band, called Burnt Lace, and they were punk, which meant a lot of eighth notes and shouting. By the luck of the draw, or the design of the universe, we were the last to go on.

Gigi and Viv were so nervous they could barely look at me, the audience or anything. I kept smiling at them as we set up because the main thing about performing live is that if you're not having fun, nobody else will. That was not from my dad; I think that was from reading some cheesy performing arts magazine, but I was using everything I could think of. However, they couldn't smile. They finally just lifted their heads, which was enough. Ella, who was never going to smile at anything, counted us in and I started playing really loud rhythm guitar and Viv started singing and the buzz in the room turned to a stunned silence. Viv had never sung better. And it was as if I were hearing the words to my own song for the very first time.

We launched with "Walking Contradiction" and then the song I'd sketched out called "Looks Like Faith," and another, barely finished, called "Keep Me Informed," then a reinterpretation of "Happy" by the Stones.

After a while my eyes adjusted and I could see Redmond standing in the audience, watching us with his arms crossed. I tried to smile at him but I wasn't sure he was looking at me. Anybody with any sense was looking at Viv. But then my eyes floated across the crowd, past my mother, who was smiling, and Ed the Guitar Guy, who had his arm draped across her shoulders, and the fancy school parents, who looked alarmed or sad, and finally they landed on Jeff. He raised his hand in a subtle wave and he was watching me with something in his eyes I wasn't sure I'd seen before and I didn't know what to do with it.

I looked down at my guitar and played it like it wouldn't behave and when I looked back up, the number was over and people were going nuts. Before we even started the next number, I knew we had won.

Only we hadn't won.

We had tied. With the Clauses.

The announcer called us up onstage and everyone clapped.

The announcer said it had been such a close call the decision was that we both qualified for the Unsigned Competition at Coachella and we were going to split a three-hundred-dollar award.

Redmond Dwayne and I shook hands and then he put his arm around me, just to upstage me. Jeff was watching. My mother was staring, her mouth in the shape of a little o. I had no idea which part was making her look that way. My news about my father, us winning Whisky, or Redmond "Sunglasses Inside" Dwayne throwing his arm around me. I suspected it was just the powerful cocktail of all of it. Ed's expression didn't change. He smiled at me the way he smiled at the world in general.

By the time we had broken down our stuff and come outside, most of the audience had cleared out. Mom gave me a stifling hug and tried to hide the fact that she was crying.

"Do you want to do the Coachella thing?" she asked.

She and Ed exchanged a look, as if this had been discussed in my absence.

"Of course I do."

"Then I think you should. I wish you could promise me that you won't fall in love with the whole thing. You'll keep your options open. Will you?"

"She can't promise a thing like that," Ed the Guitar Guy said.

"It's not even me," I said to reassure her. "It's Viv they're responding to."

"But they're your songs," Mom said. "The songwriter is everything."

"I wish you'd figure out where you stand on this," I said.

"I wish I would, too," she admitted with a smile.

"You know the richest people in the music industry are people you can't see. The songwriters. Diane Warren, people like that," Ed said.

"This isn't about getting rich," I told them.

"Well, that's mostly true," Ed the Guitar Guy said, "of every artist. But sometimes it happens and you have to run with it."

I was about to engage in that bizarre discussion when I saw Jeff lingering by the door.

"Excuse me for a minute," I said to them.

"It's your night," my mother said, making a sweeping gesture.

Jeff watched me walk toward him with a smug expression.

When I arrived he bowed and said, "What can I say?"

"You can say congratulations."

"Well, that," he said.

"What else?"

"You were inspiring."

"Who did we inspire? Everybody who lost got pissed and left."

"I didn't."

"You weren't in the game."

"Of course I was. I was your roadie and I inspired your song."

"Look at you, trying to lap up the spotlight."

"Might as well. Given how much you hate it."

"I don't hate it," I said, turning my face away from him, to hide how much I was blushing.

"Good. You should be proud."

"Pride goeth before a fall," I said.

"No. Pride goeth before a burger. If you'll join me for one."

I laughed. "I can't. I have to go home."

"Why?"

"I have to study. I'm a student. Music is a hobby. I'm not really an artist."

"Like hell you aren't."

He made me feel happy and I stopped myself from tickling his chin, which was suddenly a weird thing I wanted to do.

"What do you know about it? It's all numbers in your universe."

"Numbers are art," he said. "Let me correct your false impression, Street. Numbers are language. And it's not the language I love, it's the system they represent."

"Thanks, Teacher."

"Sure you don't want that hamburger?"

"Well, I do but I can't. My mom. You know."

"Okay. Next time, rock star. Go with your mom. I'll take your stuff back to Peace. It'll be safe there."

"Thanks, Jeff."

"Your loyal roadie. See you in the salt mines," he said, and he leaned in and gave me a kiss on the cheek. I turned red and wanted to faint. In front of all those people.

I walked toward my gear and I saw Redmond in the very back of the room next to our stuff.

He was engaged in talking to Viv.
I said, "Excuse me," and started winding cable.
Viv giggled and they moved aside.
"See you at Coachella," Redmond said.
"Don't lose any sleep over it," I suggested.
I could have sworn he winked.

Winter Breakdown

School let out for winter break.

Mom and ETG had talked about crazy stuff like going skiing or to Vegas but that fit of craziness passed when Mom realized she had to put in more hours at Biscuit. Louise had fallen apart because Married Man had decided not to leave his wife (again).

"Right here at the holidays," Mom said. "Couldn't she pick another time to fall apart?"

"Everybody does it at the holidays," Ed said. "It's a tradition."

All these hours at the store left me and Ed kicking it at home, eating macaroni and cheese and watching reality programs.

"Do you have a place, Ed, or do you live here now?"

"I have an apartment. But I like to be here when Diane comes home."

"You don't stay over."

"Right."

"Because of me?"

"Uh-huh."

"Because you think I don't know you're having sex?"

"Well, I'll tell you, Blanche, my sex life is none of your business."

I got quiet and stared at the television.

"Is this about Coachella?" he asked. "Performance jitters again or actual hostility?"

"I don't know."

He said, "Nothing's going to interfere with you being famous, Blanche, if that's what you want. Don't worry. Nothing can interfere with what people want."

"Oh, really?"

"Well, big things. Wars."

"What about my mother? Didn't something interfere with what she wanted?"

He put pepper on his mac and cheese and swirled it around. "I don't think so. She has you. She has a store. She has friends, has the program, has me."

"It's not the life she imagined for herself."

"Did you ever ask her what she imagined for herself?"

"I don't have to. I lived it."

"What are you so mad about?"

"Where do you wanna start?"

"You're mad at her because he left? That doesn't make much sense."

"Not that anymore. I'm mad at her for giving up after he left."

"Being happy with the small stuff is your idea of giving up? Something for you to think about, Blanche."

I didn't answer. We were quiet for another long spell.

Then he said, "You know, I once opened for your dad."

I felt the air leaking out of my lungs.

"Opened what?" I finally asked.

He said, "Troubadour. I was friends with the booker there. We used to drink together. Anyway, the booker said to me, come open for this guy, Duncan Kelly. He's the next big thing."

I looked at him. "Did you do it?"

"Sure, of course I did."

I forgot about breathing.

"Did you talk to my dad?"

He shrugged. "I think we said hello backstage. Your mother might have even been there. We've talked about that."

I tried to wrap my head around it. While I was thinking he said, "We weren't anything special. My band, the Listless, we were called. We were kind of Eagles Light."

"Eagles Light? Isn't that like Skimmed Milk Light?"

He laughed. "The Eagles had some pretty tough guitar playing if you're willing to listen."

I said, "Did you really use the word 'tough' in relation to the Eagles?"

He laughed again.

"How's Coachella going?" he asked.

"We got confirmation the other day. We're the sixth slot

out of ten. There are bands from all over, including England and Norway."

"That's great," he said. "Is your dad coming?"

I looked at him.

"What?"

"Well, I figured that would have crossed your mind. You mentioned that you e-mailed with him."

I stared at him, at his sleepy blue eyes, and I imagined that ETG could see through me, could see all my crazy plans and secret thoughts. Maybe could see the volumes of songs I had under my mattress. He was making me very uncomfortable. Because I hadn't said a word to anyone about my real motivation behind this band thing. That if I became a musician, if I got my band into Coachella, I'd replace that thing my father had taken out of the house when he went away.

And he'd have a reason to come back. I thought if anything in the world could get him back here, it would be to see me in my own band.

This was a far dirtier secret than the notebooks under my mattress. So you can imagine how I felt about Ed the Guitar Guy getting a clue.

"I don't know what you're talking about," I said to him.

"Okay."

Ed had a way of doing that. He had a way of deflating all my big ideas with his calm acceptance of them. How could I work with a guy like that?

I had more to say on the subject but the door opened and my mother came in. She was energized and happy, talking about all the coats and sweaters and bangles they had sold. Ed the Guitar Guy watched and listened as if he'd never heard a story so good, or seen anyone so enchanting. Without looking at me he stood and went to my mother and they hugged, and over his shoulder, she looked at me as if to say, *Sorry for hugging a guy who isn't your father.*

"I'm tired, so, good night," I said.

I went to my room and for a long time I tried to read or play the guitar or write in my journal so I could pretend I wasn't going to do what I was always going to do.

I started the e-mail:

> Hello Pater,
> We won the concert at the Whisky. Well, tied, actually. But now we're going to play in the Unsigned Competition at Coachella. If Hawaii gets boring, think about checking it out. I don't know if they had it when you were here but it's the most famous music festival in the country. And the Fringers, my band, are on the bill.
>
> If you can't, I'll e-mail pictures but it would be awesome to see you.
>
> It's in late April so you have lots of time to plan.

I sent it and then I sat still for a long time and tried to feel that idea moving halfway around the globe. In the next room, Mom was laughing and Ed was talking in his nasally Midwestern tones.

I didn't tell my father anything about the prayer box or

my confusion over being an artist. I still wasn't one, as far as I was concerned. I was just a critic playing around in the sandbox of creativity.

I knew what he'd say to me.

He'd say that being an artist was nothing to fool around with.

But I knew something else he had never told me. Wanting to be an artist didn't have to be a prescription for your demise.

Owning it was something else.

It made me sleepy to think about it all so I lay down on my bed, still in my clothes, and gave in to the dreams that were banging at the door behind my eyes. It's what you do when you run out of options.

TECHNICAL PROBLEMS

Christmas Eve

My mother dragged us to Midnight Mass. Even though she wasn't a traditional believer, and Ed was a lapsed Catholic, she said she'd always wanted to go and she was a big fan of ritual and hymns and people getting together to think good thoughts.

I'd been in a Catholic church twice before. Once at a wedding and once when my mother was exploring world religions. She took me to a Mass and a Buddhist temple and a prayer circle and to see some whirling dervishes at UCLA and I don't know what all. They eventually ran together for me. It all looked like a bunch of people being incredibly excited about something invisible. So even though I'd seen a Mass before, when we went on Christmas Eve, there was something different about it. Maybe it was that I was in the grips of my dreams, the excitement surrounding Coachella, the songs that were bouncing around in my head, waiting to be written, and the hope of hearing back from my father. He hadn't answered my e-mail yet but I imagined that was because he was just thinking of something to say. The point was, the world felt all swollen with possibility and magic didn't seem that far off.

The church was lit entirely by candles and the organ music filled it, somber and beautiful, and the incantations that all the people said together had an effect on me. I stood in the pew next to my mother and Ed the Guitar Guy, and I looked at all the people around us and the priest in his robe and the altar boys holding candles on long sticks and all the haunting, scary but strangely beautiful statues around and something stirred in me. I won't tell you that I became a believer. But in that moment, I was thinking, *What if it's true?* What if the thing they are talking about isn't entirely invisible but just circulating and moving and pulsating in a place our eyes simply aren't trained to see? What if it's like sound waves, the things that came out of my guitar and Gigi's bass and Ella's drums and Viv's voice, these great vibrations that didn't exist and suddenly did, and then they floated away and kept on living somewhere, if only in the memories of the people who heard them?

What if it was all part of the invisible system Jeff talked about?

Synergy, he called it. A silver network of threads holding it together, creating meaning and purpose. X's and O's.

I felt my forehead to see if I had a fever. These kinds of thoughts were not like me at all.

Another thing that happened was that I looked at Mom

and Ed and they seemed kind of right together, as if they'd known each other a very long time, like in another life. And they had finally found each other. I saw a different quality in my mother's face and her body language. There was a peacefulness to her, a settling, or a calm, like when the ocean glasses over.

Ed had put his arm across her shoulders and she leaned her head against him.

It wasn't sexual. It was friendly and united.

What was I supposed to do with that?

The thing about Santa Claus came into my brain and I told myself that this was no different. This was just a beautiful myth for adults to believe in but it was all the same thing. It was not a reality. Standing there, listening to the organ and feeling all the belief around me, I just wanted it to be true. Then I was ashamed of wanting it to be true because I couldn't imagine what my father would say about that. I couldn't imagine where he was this Christmas, how he dealt with the whole holiday. Did he spend it alone and ignore it completely? Or did he go out to Christmas luaus in Hawaii? Did he ever think of us?

I watched the people going up to take Communion. I was moved by it. It made me smile and at the same time it made tears well up. Tears that I fought back with everything I had because there was no way I was going to cry about people standing in a long line to participate in a ritual that shouldn't make any sense at all. If Jesus had been the son of God and he'd been born to spare everybody their sins, why did everyone still suffer and why did pretending to eat him in a cracker ease their suffering? Now it was a conversation

I wanted to have but I had no idea who to have it with. I stared at the serious face of the priest and couldn't imagine having it with him. I looked at my mother and I knew I'd never bring up anything so difficult with her. I looked at Ed and was shocked when I realized I could have that conversation with him.

I watched as he walked up to take Communion. When he came back to the seat he was chewing the cracker. He winked at me before lowering the prayer bench and getting on his knees. My mother didn't kneel but stood very tall and straight beside him. And that impressed me. She didn't need to do what he was doing. She was her own person—not buying in to his Catholic tradition but not rejecting it, either.

I thought we might have a conversation when we got home but I didn't know how to bring it up. We sat in the living room and Mom made hot chocolate. We sipped and they talked about how well Biscuit was doing and how well Ed the Guitar Guy's shop was doing and that meant we might actually be able to go skiing or something in January and then Mom said, Oh, wouldn't it be nice to have some music?—Ed could borrow my guitar, and I said yes. He started playing some old songs that I happened to know so I provided harmony and Mom just sat there watching as if everything were turning out the way she'd always dreamed but never planned. It annoyed me and pleased me at the same time and I was resisting, with everything in me, the way I resisted the tears in church, feeling that this was all a good thing. Then Ed gave me presents and I opened them. He gave me some picks and some songbooks—collections of the eighties and nineties, and we looked at the chords and talked about the ones I knew and the ones I'd have to learn. I thanked him and didn't know if I should show how much I actually liked it all. Because secretly I did.

Finally Ed left. My mother and I watched the end of *A Christmas Carol* before going to bed and that was the last normal moment I had for a really long time.

My overhead light popped on around two a.m. and I said, "Mom, come on, Christmas can wait." She often got excited about things like that and couldn't resist waking me up early. "The presents will be just as much fun in two hours."

She didn't say anything. She moved into the room and said, "Come into the living room."

I could tell from her tone that she wasn't talking about opening presents.

I followed her into the living room and my heart was working very hard. There was a breaking news story on. I could barely make myself say it:

"Is it Dad?"

All my life I knew that if something bad happened to my father, we'd probably hear it on the news before we got a call. That's how it went with famous people.

"No," she said.

By then I was staring at the screen and before I heard the words I saw the crawl on the TV screen.

"Local girl lost in Angeles Forest."

"Who?" I asked my mother. "Someone we know?"

Then the reporter was talking: "The sixteen-year-old girl from West Los Angeles, a student at Laurel Hall Academy, was separated from her parents during a hiking trip late on Christmas Eve. Her parents, Drs. Hugh and Evelyn Wyler, are well-known scientists who do research in the areas of physics and biology. Their youngest daughter, Vivien, was last seen by them yesterday when she fell behind the family during their hike. So far, the search has revealed no sign of her, and we've been told that the temperatures did dip into the twenties here last night."

I looked at my mother.

"They'll find her, right? They always find people, don't they?"

"I think they do. Usually."

"But the twenties, that's not so cold. She probably found a cave."

"Probably," Mom said.

We stood staring at the screen, pictures of rescue workers and dogs and helicopters moving past, and I couldn't believe this was all going on right before my eyes, all over my friend Viv, who had stood next to me on a stage, singing my songs, just a few days before.

"What should we do?" I asked.

She didn't know the answer to that, either.

I heard my cell phone ring and grabbed it. It was Gigi.

"Oh, my God, have you turned on the TV?"

"Yes," I said. "We're watching it now."

"What can we do?" she asked.

"I don't know."

"I'm coming over. I'm gonna call Ella and we'll come over. We should all be together."

Mom called Ed the Guitar Guy and he came over. He had a friend who had a friend who was a cop in that area of the country so he called and talked to him. But the cop had no news. It was just the same as what we were hearing on the TV. The cop did say that the majority of the time they found people within twenty-four hours but there was bad weather, clouds moving in, and if it started to snow it could really set things back.

Ed and Mom and I ate eggs while we waited for my friends. We were quiet.

After a moment Mom put her face in her hands and sat there.

"Are you crying?" I asked.

"No," she said. "I was praying."

"Oh, Mom, don't."

"I didn't ask you to join me."

"It's superstition. It's ridiculous. We need to do something real."

"Hey," Ed said, precisely in the tone of a father.

"Hey, what?"

"I know you're scared," he said. "But I can't let you take it out on your mother."

I thought about taking him on and telling him he wasn't an authority figure, he was just some guy who sold guitars, but I realized this was far from the time to do that. So I backed off.

Gigi and Ella arrived and Mom made them some food and we went over all the details again. Gigi's father had talked to Viv's father and they had been walking for half an hour before they realized she wasn't with them. She was dressed well but she didn't have any food or water with her. She had a cell phone but it had died because she had mentioned that on the walk. He said the rescue workers were pretty optimistic but the weather was a real threat.

"Should we go up there?" I asked my mother.

"No, sweetie. There's nothing we can do. It would just create more stress."

We sat there looking at the news for another hour or so and then my mother said, "We have to do something. Let's go."

Ed drove us up to the Angeles Forest, which was about an hour away, and we couldn't get very close to where they were searching. They made us sit and wait in the restaurant of a lodge. We drank tea and stared out the windows at the clouds lying close to the ground. It looked and smelled like snow. I thought about how odd it was that we lived in a desert but we were just an hour away from snow. An hour away from a forest so vast that you could get lost in it and stay lost for a long time.

After a couple of hours the Wylers came in with one of their other daughters, Claire. She was a freshman at Pomona, and the only thing I knew about her was that she, like the other sister, Jasmine, was smarter than Viv. Viv said both her sisters were smart and she was the sporty one. Her parents didn't get her, she said, and worried about her all the time. I remembered telling her that nobody's parents got them; she was probably just being sensitive. But she said that wasn't the case, she really was the black sheep, but she wasn't all that bothered by it. She meant it, too. Viv didn't get emotional. Just as she didn't take it all that seriously that she had a voice most girls would kill for. Viv was centered and strong and I realized how much I had come to like her and rely on her. She would be okay. She had to be. If anyone could figure out how to survive, it had to be Viv because she wouldn't panic. She was an athlete. She understood her body and what it could do. Which was probably how she had gotten into trouble. Feeling overconfident, getting separated from the others.

The Wylers didn't say much but they were glad to see us. I realized it was helpful for us to be there. Ed talked in low tones to Viv's father. My mother just had her hand on Evelyn's shoulder. I felt for the first time, maybe ever, how much harder it was to be the adults. And I wasn't sure I could do that when it was my turn.

Gigi started to cry and Ella glared at her and said, "Cut it out, I mean it. They don't need that right now."

"You're right," Gigi said, and sucked it up. "But she's gonna be okay, right? We can't know someone who could disappear and . . ."

She didn't say "die."

Ella shook her head and stared at her Converse shoes. Her foot was swinging back and forth, fast and hard.

"It sure would be great to believe in God right now," I couldn't help saying.

Ella raised her eyes to me. "It's Christmas."

"Right. I forgot."

"How does that matter?" Gigi asked. "And who doesn't believe in God? Everybody does, even if they're not religious."

I didn't say anything more about it, about how my father had taken God out the door along with famous.

We stayed at the lodge with Viv's family. I was lying on the couch in front of the fire when my mother woke me up.

"They found her?" I asked, my heart pounding.

"No," she said. "But we have to go home. It's starting to snow."

That was the first time I felt panicked and I couldn't stop the tears that had started to well up the night before at Mass and seemed somehow related.

I didn't even fight it when Ed the Guitar guy put an arm around my shoulders and I let him lead me out to the car. Ella and Gigi followed and there was nothing to say.

Day Four

When bad things happen, the hardest thing to believe is that the machinery of life just keeps going. Everything I did made me feel guilty and strange, from brushing my teeth to watching television. It bothered me enough to say some version of it out loud to my mother.

"It was like that when your father left," she said. "I couldn't understand the whole idea of the sun rising and setting, let alone going to the grocery store or washing the dishes."

"How did it change?"

"It just does, slowly, over time."

I looked at her because she was sort of saying what everyone was afraid to say. That Viv might very well be dead. That with every day that passed, she was more likely to be dead. The rescue workers, when interviewed on TV, said they were still optimistic and that it was entirely possible for a young person to still be alive and well. She could be eating vegetation and drinking snow and there were lots of places for shelter.

We were still on winter break. Ella and Gigi and I got together the first two days but that made things worse because it just reminded us of who was missing. Then I just stayed in the house and watched the news and ate junk. Ed the Guitar Guy tried to coax me out of my worry with some music, showing me new guitar licks, and I allowed myself to get sucked in because it did give me some relief, a reasonable distraction.

But then things would happen, like getting e-mail and letters from Coachella, telling us the rules and guidelines and asking us to submit our set list for our upcoming show. They were pleased to have the Fringers join them and could we please submit the full names and addresses of all the band members and what instruments they played so they could post it on their Web site.

I went ahead with the plans because not doing it felt like saying she wouldn't be around for it. But it was hard to handle all the feelings that came up. Because I did feel disappointed that we might not make it. And then I felt horrible about that.

Then the e-mail. That made things almost unbearable.

My father had written back. It was waiting for me that Christmas night, when I got back from the Angeles Forest.

> Hey, Rock Princess,
> This is exciting news. It coincides with a
> fit of island fever. I've been thinking about

revisiting the other society and this is the perfect occasion for it. If you're serious, put me on the guest list. Maybe you could even get me backstage. Send me the dates. Love and congrats. D.

I had no idea what to do with that information. I couldn't tell my mother because I didn't want to remind her that I was still talking to him. I didn't want her to know that he might come to Coachella because I couldn't imagine what that would do to her. And I couldn't even think about the fact that none of this would come to pass, anyway, because Viv might not come back.

On day four a vigil was held for Viv at Laurel Hall. Half of the student body came back from whatever they were doing to attend. Parents came, too. Some locals who had nothing to do with the school came. Religious people and political activists and people who decided that this was all the fault of global warming. Redmond Dwayne and the Clauses came and Mom and Ed the Guitar Guy and Ella and Gigi and their parents and Jeff and the Bos from Peace Pizza. I was glad to see Jeff but I felt guilty about that. Dr. Bonny made a speech and then she turned the service over to a priest and then a rabbi and then a Buddhist monk and finally to a grief counselor. We lit candles and we sang and afterward I didn't feel like much had been accomplished. Ella and Gigi and I talked about hanging out at somebody's house afterward but we didn't have any enthusiasm for it. We had seen each other every day and it wasn't helping.

Walking to the car with Mom and Ed, I heard someone

calling after me. I turned and watched Jeff catching up to me. His cheeks were red from running.

"Street," he said. "Do you want to go for coffee or something? And then I'll take you home."

"I guess not," I said.

"Honey, it might help," Mom said.

"How would it help?"

"Get your mind off of things," Ed said.

"I don't want my mind off of things." I turned to Jeff and said, "I'm sorry, I don't mean to be rude, it just doesn't seem like the best time."

He nodded. And yet I couldn't move. He said something to my mother. The next thing I knew he was leading me by the shoulders and then I was inside his Volkswagen Jetta and before he could start the engine I was crying harder than I could remember crying since maybe the first grade when my dad left. Jeff sat very still and didn't try to touch me or say anything. My nose was running and I wiped it on my sleeves until Jeff gave me a handkerchief. It had his initials on it.

"I never took you for a guy with initialed handkerchiefs."

He shrugged. "Walking contradiction."

"Do you keep them around for when girls cry?"

"My mom gives them to me. She's old school. I can't give them back, it would hurt her feelings. So I keep them."

"You are a conundrum," I said.

"Yeah. So are you."

"Yeah?"

"You write those songs and you get up there onstage and you let people see all sides of you. But not you. Not really."

"I just cried and wiped my nose in front of you."

"I'm going to savor this moment," he said.

"Okay, take me for coffee, gearhead, or take me home."

We went to a place around the corner from the school and across the street from the Guitar Center and the Indonesian shop where we'd made offerings to the prayer box. Every now and then he said something about how sure he was they were going to find her, and if you thought about it, four days wasn't that long. He knew all kinds of stories about people being found after two or three weeks.

"Viv's smart, right?" he said.

"Yes and no."

"Her parents are scientists."

"She's a jock. I mean, she's not stupid, but I don't know if we can rely on her survival skills. She's a great singer, that's what she is. I'd love to have her talent. I mean, not her talent, that's hers. I'd like to have a voice like hers."

"But then you wouldn't have a voice like yours."

"That's no loss to the world."

He turned his head, a kind of puppy head cock.

"Is this an act?" he asked.

"Is what an act?"

"You don't know how cool you are."

"Don't be ridiculous. I don't even know what color my hair is."

"It's striped," he said. "That's not a plan?"

"Nothing is a plan, Jeff. Everything's random."

"If you understood numbers, you wouldn't say that."

I put my head in my hands. "Really? Right now?"

He leaned across the table and made me look up.

"I quit smoking," he said.

"That was a short hobby."

"It was stupid. It was to make you notice me."

"How could I not notice you? You work with me."

He shook his hair out of his face. He must have known I liked that gesture.

He said, "Here's my dirty secret. I love the whole world of X's and O's talking to each other and—"

"Jeff, that's not a secret."

"Let me finish. And to me, it's like art. The way we create these systems striving for perfection, connecting us all. Hardly anyone else sees it as art. Well, at MIT or Caltech, but like you, they see it as geekdom. I didn't think I could ever get you or anyone to see me as anything but that."

"So what do you want me to do? Officially declare, 'You are not a geek'?"

"I just want you to see me."

"I see you. I don't know what you mean by that."

He opened his mouth and closed it again. As if he had run out of words.

My phone rang. I glanced down at the number. It was my mother's.

"Hold that thought," I said.

I knew what it was before I answered it.

"They found her," I said.

"Yes. She's going to be okay."

And for the second time I started blubbering right in front of Jeff.

Then It Gets Weird

"When people die or nearly die, they get instantly popular. It's the glamour, the thing that sets you apart and makes people want to form a connection."

This was something my father said on the occasion of the death of some rock legend that he happened to know. He explained to me in an e-mail that the guy was marginally talented and never very likable but now he was going to "get perfect." He said, "Make sure you don't count on death as your backup plan."

I didn't think that made my dad as weird as it might have sounded. He was a poet; he saw things that way and he couldn't help sharing them. And I liked that he never filtered his ideas for me. He talked to me as if I'd always been capable of hearing things like that. And in a way, as if I was more capable than my mother.

But the point is, he was so often right.

We went to the hospital and it was nearly impossible to find a place to sit in the waiting room. Now Viv was a rock star.

Gigi and Ella and I hugged each other and talked very quickly and it took a while to get annoyed about not getting to see her. We waited patiently along with so many of the people who'd been at the vigil, including Redmond Dwayne, and all the parents, and Jeff, who had driven me directly there. He leaned against the wall, smiling at me from across the room. He was giving me space. He'd probably read about doing that.

It was close to nine when my mother came in and said, "Visiting hours are almost over. We should probably go home."

"What? Not see Viv?"

She said, "Her parents are with her. She has a lot of visitors, even the press. We can come back tomorrow."

"It's not fair," I said. "We're her band."

She put a hand on my shoulder and said, "She's going to be around for a while. We can come back."

"Yeah, okay," I said. I had momentarily forgotten my gratitude.

I was saying goodbye to Gigi and Ella when a nurse entered the waiting room and said, "Is there a Blanche out here? A Blanche Kelly?"

I turned and raised my hand as if I were in school. The nurse pointed a clipboard at me.

"You're Blanche?"

"Yes."

"She wants to see you. Visiting hours are really over, so everybody else go home."

Mom and Ed had to stay behind and I followed the nurse down a corridor, into an elevator and down another corridor. It was late and people were leaving, in various states of emotion.

Finally we arrived at Viv's room. Her parents and sisters were standing outside. They were talking and smiling. When they saw me, her parents hugged me and her mother said, "She is very insistent upon talking to you, Blanche."

"I'm happy she's okay," I said.

"Yes, we're all relieved," her mother said. She gestured toward the door and I went in alone.

Viv was lying in the hospital bed, propped up on some pillows, staring at the blank TV screen as if she were waiting for something to appear on it. She sat straight up when I came in and a smile took over her face. She patted the bed next to her and I sat down. I hugged her. She felt very skinny.

She said, "Have you been here long?"

"Awhile. A lot of people were in the waiting room."

"The doctors gave me all these tests. Then I had to talk to the reporters. You'd think I'd invented something."

"Are you okay?"

"I am now. I was hungry but they let me eat some stuff. Not too much. They say you can't eat a lot at once after you nearly starve."

"You nearly starved?"

"Well, they say so. I wasn't hungry much after the first day. I was just cold."

"Do you have frostbite or anything?"

She shook her head. "I found this place under a rock and I made a bed with some leaves and limbs and stuff. I was near a stream so I drank water. I saw something on the Discovery Channel that said you're not supposed to move far from where you get lost. So I just stayed in the same place for a while."

"What did you do?"

"That's what I want to talk to you about." She smiled.

"Go ahead."

"The first two days were really bad. I was afraid and I worried and I was hungry and cold and stuff. But eventually I got tired and I slept a lot. Then around day three, something happened. I want to tell you."

"Tell me," I said.

She was holding my hand now, gripping it pretty tight.

She said, "I thought I was probably going to die. And a lot of stuff went through my head. Believe it or not, I was sorry that we wouldn't make Coachella, that was the first thing. The second thing, stupid as it sounds, was that crazy guy Redmond Dwayne."

"He was here," I said. "He was at the vigil and again in the waiting room."

She waved a dismissive hand. "He doesn't matter. I was just missing all the things I thought I'd have. But I got to this weird place where I was ready to die. I don't mean ready. I mean I figured it was going to happen so it was kind of like when you take an exam. You're sitting at your desk and the teacher is passing it out and you know you've wasted some time but you've also studied a little and you're just hoping you've done more of one than the other. When you think you're going to die, this weird thing kicks in where you start focusing on the part where you studied. That is, the good stuff you did. And I was thinking about the talent show and how awesome that was and how happy I was that I had it to think about when I was about to die. I was thinking how kind of sad my life might have been without it. At least I did that. That was what I was thinking and I was grateful that you made me do it."

"I don't think I made you do it."

"Just listen."

"Okay."

"So on what I guess was the third day when I was getting kind of delirious and sleepy, I kept drifting off, thinking about the band and missing out on Coachella. I didn't think about soccer at all. I mean, sometimes I had these crazy dreams about missing goals and stuff. But those were mostly nightmares. The nice dreams were about the band. I got to this place . . . and it's hard to explain . . . but I got to this place where all I could think about was the band and every time I thought about it, I felt happy enough to die. And it was while I was feeling like that, I started to pray."

"Pray," I said.

"Yeah. You know, my parents are scientists and we don't believe in that stuff. But I thought, why not try it out. So I prayed. I didn't pray for anything specific. I just got very quiet and thought about help."

"Okay."

"Nothing happened at first. Then I fell asleep and when I woke up, I was looking at this . . . I don't know, Blanche . . .

this thing. It looked like a person but it was more shiny. It was like a white shiny shape. I couldn't make out any features because it was just so bright. It was like looking at a sunrise. You want to stare but you can't. I had this overwhelming feeling that whatever it was, it was good news. Not like death. It was some other kind of news. And it kind of spoke to me."

"It spoke. The white shiny thing."

"Yeah. Not with words but with thoughts. My thoughts could hear its thoughts or something."

"Okay."

"Do you know what it said to me?"

"No," I said.

"It said, 'Don't be afraid.' "

"Oh. Like in the Bible?"

"I don't know. I don't read the Bible."

"In the Bible, angels are always saying don't be afraid."

"Well, I'm not saying it was an angel. Necessarily."

"Okay, go on."

"It said, 'Remember what you prayed for the first time.' "

"You prayed for something?" I asked. "When? You said you didn't pray before."

She leaned forward and squeezed my hand harder.

She said, "The prayer box."

"The prayer box."

"When we went to that weird shop that day, next to Guitar Center."

"Oh, the prayer box."

"Yes," Viv said. "The thing, whatever it was, said, 'Remember what you prayed for.' "

"Oh," I said.

"And at first I couldn't remember what I prayed for. When we did the prayer box thing, I thought it was all kinda stupid. Remember, we wrote down our prayers but I was just goofing around. I didn't know what to put."

"Right," I said.

"So I jotted something down. I wrote down, 'Safe from harm.' "

I just looked at her.

"Safe from harm," she repeated. "Why would I put that? I couldn't even imagine being in any kind of danger. I just put it down without thinking about it."

"That's not so strange, Viv. People always pray for health and safety."

"You didn't, did you?"

I thought about it. It was true, I hadn't.

And Gigi had prayed to win the talent contest. No telling what Ella had prayed for.

But my prayer hadn't been serious. And I hadn't expected anyone's to be. The outing had been no more meaningful to me than going to a coffee place. I had to believe that Viv was just dreaming, just suffering from some strange aftereffect of nearly dying.

Her eyes were bearing down on me, though, and I felt she was expecting me to realize something of great importance. I just kept holding her hand and I waited.

"My prayer was answered," she said.

"Okay," I said.

"Blanche, don't you get it? It's all real. That whole idea of God. It's not a dream."

"Okay, Viv."

She stared at me for a moment and then her face changed. She let go of my hand and lay back down on her pillows.

"You don't believe me," she said.

"I don't not believe you," I said. "I just don't know what to think."

She lay there for a moment, then sat back up.

"So let me tell you the rest of it."

"Go ahead," I said.

She cleared her throat and said, "The way they found me. Do you know about the way they found me?"

"No," I said.

"My cell phone had died so I couldn't call anyone. I kept checking it right after I got lost but it wouldn't even turn on. But after that dream, or whatever it was, I woke up because my cell phone was making a noise. Like an alarm. I woke up and my cell phone was on and blinking. I couldn't believe it. I started dialing numbers. At first it just bleeped but finally I called my mother and she answered and I started talking to her. I told her where I thought I was. And the cell phone stayed on and the rescue people, they started picking up my signal. I kept talking on the phone until finally it died and about two minutes after it died, there was a helicopter and they somehow saw me. And I was rescued. I picked up my phone again to talk to them but it was completely dead. Like it had always been dead. When I checked my log of sent calls, it hadn't recorded any of the time I spent talking to my mother. It was dead from the time it died, you know? It's like it never happened except it did."

I didn't know what to make of any of this. I just sat very still, listening to Viv.

We were quiet for a while and I could tell she was waiting for some kind of reaction to her story but I didn't have one.

She was staring at me and then she collapsed into the pillows again.

"I thought you'd understand," she said. "You of all people."

"Why me?" I asked.

"Because you're the one who got me to pray. You're the one who led me to the prayer box."

I shook my head. "It was just a game. The prayer box. I didn't really think . . . It was like wishing on candles."

"It wasn't like that," she said. "That's what I'm trying to tell you."

"Listen, on Christmas Eve I went with Mom and Ed the Guitar Guy to church. When I was sitting there with all the candles and the music, I started to think it might be real, the whole God thing. It had that effect on me. But then when I walked out, I realized I had just been imagining things. Wishful thinking. I'm fine now. You will be, too."

She lay down and turned over on her side, away from me. "Never mind. I want to go to sleep now."

"Viv, I don't think it matters how you were rescued. The important thing is you're okay. We were all so worried."

"I'd like to sleep now," she repeated.

I touched her arm but she twisted away from me and turned more on her side.

I felt like I'd let her down. No, I knew I had let her

down. But what was I supposed to do with all that information?

I stood up and said, "Good night. I'll come back tomorrow with Gigi and Ella."

She didn't answer.

I didn't say what I was thinking and hoping—that by then she'd be back to normal. She would forget the white shiny presence and the prayer box and this would all be what it really was. A bad thing that nearly happened but somehow turned out all right.

Even Weirder

School started again and we decided it was okay for our singer to have a bizarre story about an angel saving her life. I argued that it was practically a requirement for the singer to be a little unhinged. I listed a lot of examples from Billie Holiday to Björk. In fact, it was probably a good thing that Viv now had this flighty, creative side. Maybe she could participate in the songwriting and I wouldn't have to feel like that part was all on my shoulders.

Initially, I hadn't told the others. I had intended to keep it to myself. But Viv wouldn't shut up about it. She stuck to the story and told everyone who would listen. She had gone from being noncommittal about the white shiny thing and had turned it into a definite messenger from beyond.

"The crazy singer theory is an interesting one," Gigi said. "But I'm still holding on till Viv comes to her senses."

But that wasn't what happened. Viv just became more adamant about her story. She wrote about it in her English class and she submitted the essay to the *Manifesto*. Josh Hammer showed it to me when I stopped by to drop off my latest piece for "Perspective, People." I had chosen to write about the Faces, a greatly ignored British band, whose songs my father liked. I also wrote about Coachella and the Unsigned Competition. It was a little bit self-serving but it was music and it was news.

Josh pulled me aside and said, "Do you know about this whole angel thing with Viv?"

"Oh. Yeah. How did you know?"

He showed me the essay. It was pretty much what she had told me, written in plain prose. Something about the minimalist style made it seem even crazier than when I heard it in the hospital.

"Was she nutty before?" Josh asked me.

"No, she wasn't nutty. And she's not nutty now. Lots of people think they see angels. Doesn't *Newsweek* do a story about that every other month? Reporting on how many people believe in God and angels, something like seventy percent of people? You and I, we're in the minority."

Josh just blinked at me. "She said the angel talked to her."

"She never actually calls it an angel."

"And it made her cell phone work."

"Crazier stuff has happened. Lots of them. You believe in time flaps, don't you, Josh? As a nerd, aren't you required to?"

"Sure," he said, without taking offense. "But there's a scientific explanation for those. Angels? That's nuts."

That was pretty much how everyone felt. But Viv wouldn't back down and wouldn't shut up.

Her parents were even more disturbed than her friends. You can imagine. Famous scientists whose daughter was now giving regular interviews to local newspapers and TV stations about her angel encounter. (It didn't matter that she never called it an angel; the press was filling in the blank.) She was dubbed Angel Girl. Viv found it not the least bit disturbing and she didn't even put up a protest when her parents sent her to a therapist.

"Of course they're doing that," she told me. "They have to because until you've seen that dimension of life, it seems crazy. I understand."

"Viv," I said, trying to sound calm and nonjudgmental. "Everybody gets that this happened to you and you really believe it, but is it necessary to talk about it?"

"Why wouldn't I talk about it?"

"Because it's freaking people out."

"I know. That's going to have to be their problem, though."

It was our problem. And it was about to become an even bigger problem.

The first thing that happened was that Gigi stopped talking to her.

It started with an argument at lunch. We were eating outside in our usual spot and I was desperately trying to talk about school or anything except Viv's experience. But Gigi couldn't leave it alone. She kept saying, "How can you believe that? You're smarter than that. You've been raised to think scientifically."

"It doesn't matter how I was raised," Viv said, nibbling on bread. She nibbled now. Everything she did was different, softer, quieter, and stranger. "What matters is my experience."

"Don't you see how it could have been a hallucination?"

"I can see how you could think that."

"You guys," Ella said. "Can we table it? It's hard to chew and swallow when you're yelling."

"I'm not yelling," Gigi yelled.

"Okay, when you're talking enthusiastically in a loud voice," Ella said.

"I'm just making a point. Angels don't come down and save people and fix their problems."

"Hey, they came down and fixed hers, so leave it alone."

"I didn't say it was an angel," Viv reminded us.

"But why her? Why didn't they come down and fix all those people in New Orleans's problems during Katrina? Why don't they fix global warming? Why didn't they fix my mother's problem so she didn't have to leave me in a basket in a hospital parking lot?"

"I don't know," Viv said quietly. "I don't have to know the answer to that."

"Well, I have to know the answer to that," Gigi said.

"Then you should pray about it."

"I don't think I can have a friend who tells me to pray about it."

Viv didn't argue with that. She just smiled.

Ella said, "Why do her beliefs have to square with your beliefs?"

"Why are you defending her?" She turned to me. "And why aren't you contributing?"

"I don't know what to say."

"You're just trying to keep the band together."

"We're close to Coachella. Let's just talk about other things till then. Like music. I think we can survive for a couple of months and then we don't have to like each other anymore. Lots of bands do that."

"Okay, but I have to warn you, I don't think I can have actual conversations with her," she said, talking about Viv as if she weren't there.

Viv just smiled.

Gigi pulled at her hair again and left.

"Guidance told me this was going to happen."

"What?" I asked, unable to stifle the incredulous tone.

"Yeah, she said no one would believe me. Or he. Spirits don't really have a gender, turns out. Anyway, part of what she or he told me was that."

"In actual words, she or he said no one was going to believe you."

"No, with her or his mind. It's hard to explain."

"Please stop trying."

"I'll try, Blanche, but it's hard."

Coachella and the band weren't just a hobby to me, a fun preoccupation. It was the thing that was going to bring my father back into my life. Not quite the same as being rescued from the jaws of death by an angel. But to me, in a lot of ways, just as unlikely.

"Let's rehearse tonight," Ella said. "I'll text Toby and

get the room. As soon as we start playing again, it'll feel normal."

"Good idea," I said.

We stopped in the hallway before heading our separate ways and I had to ask:

"You kind of believe her, don't you?"

"If it were true, wouldn't life be more interesting?" she asked.

"That's not a reason to believe something."

She shrugged. "More than most people need."

"Okay, let me ask you something. What did you put in the prayer box?"

"You can't ask me that."

"Why not?"

"The rules are you don't tell anybody."

"I just need to know if you think it came true."

"Too soon to tell," she said. "World peace."

"Very original, Miss America."

"Look, let me ask you something," Ella said, her face softening. "Why couldn't prayers and wishes be like the same thing? Sometimes if you want it hard enough, it kind of happens. Power of positive thinking and all that. Couldn't you call it angels?"

"Ella. What you're talking about is superstition."

"How do you know?"

I shrugged. I didn't know, of course. And I had a flash of the feeling I had in church on Christmas Eve. That seductive feeling that all that faith and all those prayers and all that willingness to believe somehow had the power to make things happen.

I shrugged it off before Ella could see the doubt in my face.

"Okay," I said. "When we achieve world peace, you can say you told me so."

"It's a date," she said.

She punched my arm and walked away.

Crazy Goes to College

Another article came out about Viv in the Santa Monica newspaper and it mentioned the band, the Fringers, and the fact that I was Duncan Kelly's daughter.

The last line of the article was: "If Vivien Wyler's vision was true, the Fringers are not just a band to watch. They have been touched by angels."

"Great. Now we're all nuts," Gigi said.

"We can use this," I told them. "Anything that gets publicity for the band is a good thing."

"Oh, really," Gigi said, "then why don't we all go get arrested?"

"Be serious."

"I am serious. I couldn't be more serious."

We were sitting at rehearsal at the back room of Peace Pizza, waiting for Viv.

"I don't want our band to be the touched-by-an-angel act if it's all the same to you," Gigi said. "You forget that the band is just a hobby for me. I have plans. I'm running for school office at the end of the semester. And not on the angel ticket."

"This isn't going to interfere with your political career."

"Well, you say that, but we were just doing it for the talent show to begin with and now we're playing at Coachella," Gigi argued.

Ella was sitting behind her drum kit, inspecting her fingernails.

"Do you have an opinion about this?" I asked.

"I'm of the opinion that we should just rehearse," she said.

"What about Viv?"

"We can rehearse till she gets here."

"I wonder if her chariot got stuck in traffic," Gigi said.

I decided this was as good an occasion as any to introduce my great plan for Coachella.

"Since the cat is out of the bag about my father, and since we have to do whatever we need to do to beat the Clauses, I think we should cover one of his songs."

They stared at me. I hadn't really talked to my friends about my father. They knew who he was, because now everyone did, but they never brought it up. Probably because until this moment, I didn't want anyone to bring it up.

"I don't know any of your father's songs," Gigi said.

So I told her. On his most famous album *Ineffable* (much irony to be mined there, for sure) there was a song that got a lot of radio play called "Glass Half Shattered."

Here was the chorus:

You're staring at me like there's something to see,
Like there's an important man waiting to be set
free,
But I'm not the only man who has ever mattered,
I'm not half full or half empty, I'm a glass half
shattered.

I had downloaded it from the Internet, along with some reviews that called him a visionary, someone who spoke the hard truth even when no one was listening.

When I read those lyrics I thought about my mother, trying to make him happy and failing because he was always a glass half shattered. I vaguely remembered the song reverberating through the house when I was small.

The girls read all the lyrics and it was quiet for a spell.

I said, "It's not hard, it's just in the key of C. It's one-four-five, with a minor in the bridge, four-four time. We can play it at any tempo. I'll change it to make it from a girl's point of view, obviously. I think it could get the right kind of attention."

"What kind of attention is that?" Gigi asked. "I thought there was no wrong kind of attention."

"Look, Gigi, I don't want to fight. I just figure if you enter a competition, you should try to win. You should use what you've got."

"Doesn't that feel manipulative?"

"I don't know. Isn't every kind of show manipulative? We're trying to perform something."

"In the old days you didn't want people to know about him," Gigi said.

In the old days, I didn't have a sense of competition, of realizing there was a way to win at this. In the old days, I didn't think I had a chance of earning my father back, but I didn't say that.

"What's gotten into you?" I asked.

Gigi shook her head and pinched her lip. "I never expected it to get this far. I'm not really a bass player. We're developing fans—just look at the Joshes and Bos. And I don't think I can live up to it."

"Look, we're doing it, aren't we? It's scary to put yourself out there but somebody has to. It's about willingness."

Ella said, "Can we just hear the song?"

I played and sang them a rough version on the guitar and they listened with wide eyes. They were very still when I finished and then Ella figured out a tempo and Gigi followed along and I could see that my plans were falling into place.

Then Viv walked in.

"Sorry I'm late," she said.

"No problem," Ella said. Odd that she would end up being the peacekeeper. "We're just figuring out one of Blanche's dad's songs. You'll like it. It'll be fun to sing. Just listen."

Viv waved a hand at her and said, "I can't stay. My parents are waiting in the car. I just came by to tell you that I can't be in the band anymore."

The air seemed to get sucked out of the room and all of us were very still.

"What do you mean?" I finally said.

"Well, I don't expect any of you to understand. But ever

since my experience, I've been getting a lot of Guidance, and it's not right for me to remain in the band. I'm not sure why, but I must listen to the Guidance these days."

I looked at her. "By guidance, I assume you're not talking about Dr. Morleymower."

Viv laughed. "No. Actual Guidance. Divine Guidance."

Gigi threw her hands up and said, "This is what I'm talking about."

Ella said, "Everybody calm down. Viv, have you really thought this through?"

"I can't sing," she said. "It's not right for me. I don't know why but I'm being told I shouldn't."

I put my guitar down and moved toward her. She didn't back up; she just stood there watching me.

I said, "Viv, think about it. If you want to make this about God, why would He give you the gift of singing, and why would He rescue you from possible death, only to tell you not to sing?"

To my surprise, she just smiled at me. She said, "I don't ask God what He's up to anymore. I just do what I'm told."

"There's the slightest chance that you're still not fully recovered," I suggested.

That's when she started backing away from me.

"Oh, is that what you think? I'm crazy and I just had a crazy experience?"

"No, I'm not saying that. I'm just wondering . . ."

"I know what you're wondering. Everyone's wondering. It's why my parents are making me see a therapist, but I know what I know. Nothing is going to change that."

"You might not entirely know what you know," I said. "I

mean, that was a big ordeal and you might not be finished with . . . recovering."

"What happened to me was real. It was more real than anything that has ever happened. I know I can't do anything to convince anyone. But I do know what happened. I told myself, if it fades, I'll know it wasn't what it seemed like. But it doesn't fade. It just gets stronger."

The Bos and even Jeff had gathered at the door and were looking and listening.

"I enjoyed our time together but now I have to go," she said.

I moved toward her.

"Viv, wait. Maybe this is your parents?"

She laughed. "My parents? They want me to be in the band. They've done a complete turnaround. I have to be the first girl in the history of high school to defy her parents by not being in a rock band."

"But we need you," I said.

She shook her head. "You really don't."

Before I could argue further she just gave us a hand flip of a wave and walked out of the room. One of the Bos followed her out and then came running back into the room.

"It really was her parents waiting for her. Not a spaceship."

"Get out of here," I said, and he scrambled off, giggling.

The rest of us didn't speak for a moment. Then Gigi started packing her bass into its case.

"Well, that's what I thought. It was always supposed to be a hobby."

"Don't go, Gigi," I said.

"Blanche, I can't dedicate my whole life to this idea."

"But you enjoyed it. Don't abandon it just because we've hit a bump in the road."

"One person's bump is another person's dead end," she said.

Gigi walked out and then Ella and I were left alone in the rehearsal space. I could hear the chords from my father's song bouncing around in my head. It was hard to believe we had gotten so close to everything. And now it was falling apart. How had that happened? So much for Jeff's perfect system idea.

Ella stood and started breaking down her drum set.

"I guess that's that," she said.

"Ella, come on. This can't be over. Coachella. Everybody's dream."

"Your dream," she said. "You dragged us into it."

"Really? That's how it is? At least have the courage to admit you wanted it. Some of it. I saw how everybody was at the Whisky. I've seen how different we all are since we started the band. You barely talked to anybody before. Gigi never did anything but study. Viv didn't even realize she was a singer. I didn't dream that for us. The dream was there. I just got everybody to see it."

Ella thought about it, twirling one of her drumsticks.

She said, "Do we really need Viv?"

"Of course we need Viv. You've heard how she sings."

She shrugged. "I also heard you sing tonight. You sing fine."

"No, I don't."

"What's the big speech you always give about willingness?"

I felt the blood rush out of my face.

"That's different."

"How's it different?"

"I can't sing, Ella. That was never the idea. I just write the songs and play them. That's not enough?"

"Right now it's not. Considering."

"Even if I agreed to do that, we've lost our bass player."

"It's Gigi. You can talk her back in."

I watched Ella packing up her kit. My thoughts rolled around in my head like marbles.

"Maybe there's someone else," I said. "From Madrigals. One of the Chelseas."

"Yeah, right," Ella said.

"Anybody but me," I pleaded.

"It was just an idea," she said. "We're back where we started. Find a singer and then we'll talk."

And she walked out with her gear, leaving me a glass half shattered.

Spinning Plates

I didn't e-mail my father about Viv's angel encounter and her sudden decision to drop out. I just kept talking about how exciting the band was and how great our set list was coming. I also didn't tell him that we were going to do one of his songs because that was going to be my special surprise to him. Before I realized that my special surprise to him was going to be dropping out of the Coachella lineup.

One reason I didn't tell him was that I didn't believe it. A lot of people were invested in us going to Coachella and in Viv singing there. LaHa had gotten a little famous about it, since the only other local band attending was the Clauses. (And, of course, because we had Divine Inspiration on our side.) But never in the history of LaHa had we beaten out all the monster schools to land a spot in a major competition. The *Manifesto* had run a piece on the band, separate from the issue of Viv being touched by an angel, and Dr. Bonny had made an announcement at school and had sent letters to our homes congratulating us. That made Gigi's parents all excited about her prospects as the future president, and even Ella's parents, who had given up on her doing anything of note, started to take her seriously.

Gigi hadn't told her parents she'd quit the band. Which made me think she really hadn't.

Mr. Carmichael volunteered to help us rehearse and Dr. Morleymower would smile when he saw me in the hall, wagging a finger and saying, "Who didn't want to join Madrigals?" Everyone was taking a little piece of the pie. What they didn't understand was that the pie had turned into crazy pie and it wasn't going to Coachella or anywhere else unless someone could talk some sense into Viv.

Valiant efforts were made. Her parents reasoned with her. Her therapist gave her tests and meditations and books to read. Even Ms. Mason, the uptight religion teacher at LaHa, sat her down and explained that angels didn't really tell people not to do things. Even when the angels appeared in the Bible, they mostly told people things that they should do and even then, it was up to the person in question. Besides, she said, angels were singers so why would they tell someone not to sing?

"Of all the arguments," Viv said, "that's the worst. Angels mainly just sing in folklore, not in the Bible, and my angel, if it was an angel, didn't sing. Besides, it's not an angel telling me not to do it. It's Guidance. They are very different. The thing I saw was a being that I could see and almost touched. Guidance is more like a feeling."

This was at lunch, a few days after she walked out of rehearsal. Gigi no longer ate with us and Ella was still being cool about the whole thing. She listened as if it were fascinating information that didn't affect her directly. I had trouble holding it together. I had trouble not dropping to my knees and screaming.

I said, calmly but in a tight voice, "Did Guidance ever consider that other band members have something riding on this? Is Guidance only concerned with your well-being?"

She shrugged. Nibbling. "I don't ask Guidance questions. I just do what I'm told."

"Well, if you should ever feel like asking Guidance a question, allow me to pass that one along."

Viv wouldn't budge and I couldn't bring myself to break the news to my father. He was making travel plans.

He e-mailed again:

> Your mother is going to be okay with me showing up? I haven't talked to her in a long time.

I shot back:

> She'll be fine, she's moved on.

I was surprised and wondered if he still cared when he instantly replied:

> She has a boyfriend?

I thought about what to answer and quickly wrote back:

Not really. Just this guy who comes around.

He didn't let it drop. He asked five seconds later:

What guy who comes around?

I decided to make it less than it was.

A guy who sells guitars. They seem to be just friends.

There was a two-day lapse before he wrote again. Then he didn't reply. And when he did, he'd dropped the subject of my mother altogether.

I've forgone the idea of camping. I'll probably stay in a local hotel. But I don't want to tell anyone where. Let's keep my whole presence there a secret, okay? I'm there to see you perform, not draw attention to myself.

I hit each letter carefully:

Sure. Nobody knows and nobody needs to.

* * *

Imagine my surprise when my mother knocked on my door a few evenings later and wanted to have another one of our talks.

"Honestly, Mom," I said. "I have a lot on my mind."

"So do I."

She walked over to my bed and sat without invitation. "When were you planning to tell me about your father, Blanche? Answer me that."

I felt naked in public.

"What?" I looked around the room in a panic, as if I could somehow distract her with another subject.

"Your father is planning to come to Coachella. I now know."

"I don't really think he will—well, I wasn't sure yet."

She looked at me and said, "Honestly, Blanche, were you going to just let me go up there with Ed and run into him? Was that your plan?"

"I don't know. He . . . I . . . it was supposed to be a secret. How do you even know? He told me not to tell anyone."

"Well, he didn't mean me, Blanche. He meant his adoring public, not the mother of his child."

"Mom, how do you even know this?"

"Because he e-mailed me," she said. "The first I've heard from him in five years. You know that he sent letters and there were phone calls the first few years and then there was no communication. With e-mail he settled somewhere and I guess you two reconnected. I got over the idea of him e-mailing you, when I found out, because it made sense. Of course he has more to say to you than to me. He is your father. But when I saw his name in *my* mailbox, you can't imagine what it did to me, Blanche. You can't know."

"Mom, I don't get it. Are you still into him?"

"Into him?" she said incredulously. She started laughing and shaking her head and looking like she might cry all at once. "Not having your father is a hole in my life. It's a gaping wound. I wanted us to be a family. I tried so hard. I failed. So now, I don't want him back, but that doesn't mean I can stand there and eat corn on the cob next to him in the middle of the desert."

Now my mother was yelling and my mother did not yell. I didn't understand how this had all come together and turned into such a mess. Maybe I needed an angel or some Guidance to talk to and help me.

I said, "Mom, it doesn't matter. It's not going to happen."

"It is going to happen," she said. "He says he's coming. He wrote because he wanted me to be prepared. But I can't go there now, Blanche, don't you see? I can't go with you. I can't be a part of it."

"There's nothing to be part of," I yelled back.

"What do you mean?"

"I mean I'm not going. There's no Coachella because Viv talked to an angel or a spirit or something and now she doesn't want to sing."

This shut her up and I could see a thousand things going through her head at once.

"I don't know what you're saying."

"I don't know what I'm saying, either. But you don't

have to worry about anything because there's no Coachella and we can all just stay here and waste away in Santa Monica and never do another important thing, just the way you and Ed the Guitar Guy would want it. A quiet, sad, meaningless life."

Now her brain switched again. "Is that how you see me?"

"Isn't that how you see yourself?"

"No. You are harsh, Blanche. And it isn't how I see you."

"Well, it is me. I used to have nothing going for me, then I had a little something, and now I'm back to nothing."

"Blanche, it's not like you to talk this way."

"How do you know what I'm like? You just work and hang with the Twelve Steppers and Ed the Guitar Guy. You surrender to some mysterious Higher Power and make yourself okay with everything around you like you don't have a say in it. I tried to go for something. I worked really hard and it fell apart."

"I work really hard," she said quietly. "I don't just surrender and let things happen to me."

"You don't just surrender? Isn't that what the program is all about?"

"No. You surrender the things you can't control. If you'd come with me to a meeting you'd understand."

I was glad she didn't drink anymore but there was a part of me that thought she could just not drink, without all the literature and meetings to go with it.

"That's not what you did when he left? You didn't just surrender to a life without him?" I asked.

"He left, Blanche. I had to accept it. Would you rather I hadn't? Would you rather I kept drinking?"

"I don't even remember you drinking."

"That's a good thing."

"I don't know what I'd rather, Mom. I know you went from this great exciting life to working in a clothes store and dating Ed the Guitar Guy and it looks a lot like a big compromise. Like giving up. I don't want my life to end up that way."

"I haven't given up. I tried to rebuild. My life isn't boring. It's what I want."

"Then why do you still get upset when anyone mentions him? What about the hole in your life? What about the gaping wound? Can somebody around here be consistent? The whole thing is like a song out of tune."

She shook her head. "You are so much like him."

"I am? Since when?"

"Your father said he had a vision. No else could see it. He was furious all the time because no one else could see what he saw. He wanted to be special and then he was shocked by how lonely it was. How impossible to get people to walk beside him. He used to say he had no one to play with. He hated routine and the norm, but he wasn't strong enough to cope with the alternative."

"What does that even mean?"

"He felt like no one understood him. No one could follow him. Is that how you feel? A private school education, a job and friends—does that make you unhappy?"

"I don't know how I feel." I lied. Because that was exactly how I felt.

My mother tucked her hair behind her ears and pinched her nose at the bridge. She said, "I've never been propelled by those inner voices. It's just not in me. I'm not brave enough to go there."

"Brave enough to go where?"

"Wherever those voices take you. Whatever it is that makes you want to sing and play. I never heard that sound, Blanche. I tried really hard, for him. Now I'm trying for you, but I'm just a normal person. You're brave enough to go inside the whole dream. He talked brave but then he lost it and threw us away, too. He may still have his vision but at what cost? Don't let it be that way for you. Don't be like him, be yourself."

"I'm not brave," I screamed at her. Enough to raise her head and get that scared look from her eyes. "I'm not brave at all. I just act that way."

Her shoulders softened and she smiled.

"What's the difference?" she asked. "You are not running away like your father did. I know that about you."

I looked at her for a long time. My mother had finally asked me a question that shook me to the core. She thought she had the answer, but did I? I had no idea how to answer.

I got up and walked out of the house.

The way I was sure he used to do.

Ed the Guitar Guy's Guitar Place

First I walked toward the ocean but it was dark and cold and the harmless homeless people made me feel uncomfortable.

A lot of what was upsetting about the Fringers was how much I had put myself out there. In many ways I had finally shown everybody how I was able to do it. I had tried so hard. Jeff had once said it was hard to admit you wanted something. I wasn't sure what the other side of the argument was. With that thought in mind, I headed back toward Main Street and Peace Pizza. I suspected Jeff was working the late shift. I hoped so. I had taken a few weeks off to put Coachella together and I hadn't seen him in a while. I hadn't been in touch either by e-mail or by phone, and he hadn't, either.

As I approached Peace Pizza I saw through the big window that Jeff was standing at the register. He was giving change to a girl about my age. She wasn't anyone I knew. She was a normal-looking teenage girl in jeans and a T-shirt. She had straight dark hair with nothing in it and she was holding a piece of pizza in one hand and putting the change in her pocket with the other. Jeff was talking to her the way you would to a customer. I couldn't even say he was flirting with her.

It was just the image that disturbed me. A normal guy talking to a normal girl. When Jeff and I talked, for example, it probably looked like a normal guy talking to a crack hair girl whose clothes were from the Whatever's Clean collection. I felt as if I shouldn't be thinking so much about Jeff. What did I think, anyway? So what if he inspired me to write a song? So what?

Jeff might have looked up and glanced at me before I turned away. But I hurried on. He wouldn't get the chance to run after me, not that he would. He said he liked me but what could that lead to anyway?

I walked quickly along Main Street and before I knew it, I was halfway to Venice. I had gone past the fancy clothing stores, including Biscuit, and the bike shops and yoga shops and ice cream boutiques. I barely paid attention to anything I saw so it was a wonder that I ever saw the small, discreet, tasteful little neon guitar and the sign that said ED'S GUITARS. I'd never noticed it before.

The lights were on but I didn't see anyone moving around. Looking through the window, I saw there were rows and rows of beautiful guitars, all different sizes and colors. It looked like expensive candy. And the way they all lined up next to each other, you could tell that someone cared about them and wanted each one of them to have the right home.

I knew who that person was. It made me think differently about Ed.

I touched the door. I didn't mean to open it, or maybe I meant to.

I didn't honestly mean for a bell to go off when I stepped inside, though. I had hoped I could just slip in and slip out. I wanted to smell the guitars. It's hard to explain but they have a smell. And the best way I could ever describe it would be to say they smell like potential. Ambition and desire. If such things had a smell.

"Sorry, I'm just closing up," came a voice from the back.

I tried to hurry out before the voice became a person.

"Blanche," he said. "Is that you?"

He had come from a back room and was silhouetted in the light. Like one of the guitars on display.

I turned. "Ed?"

"Yeah, me."

"So this is your place?"

"Yeah, imagine that," he said. He moved forward and now took the shape of an actual person. He had some papers in his hand and keys dangled at his waist. "I'm just filing invoices. You want to play something, go ahead."

"I didn't mean to bother you."

"I'm not bothered. I was about to call your mom to see

if she wanted to grab something to eat. I didn't mean to work so late. The hazard of being in business for yourself. Nobody tells you when to quit."

"Ed, I might not call my mom right now if I were you."

"Why not?"

I opened my mouth and then I couldn't have been more surprised if a flock of geese had flown out of it. Because I started to cry.

Ed stared at me and let me cry without moving toward me or saying things would be better.

He just waited for a break in the action and said, "Let me close up and we'll go get some coffee."

We went to an Irish pub around the corner and he ordered fish and chips and I ordered a Coke and didn't say anything at first. There seemed to be local college students sloshing beer and leaning on each other and laughing out loud. Ed saw me watching them.

He said, "You'll probably want to go to college back East?"

"I don't know. I don't know what I'm going to do."

We sipped our drinks.

Finally he said, "So what's it about?"

I shrugged. "What's what about?"

He said, "Why don't we just not do the part where I have to drag it out of you?"

"Hey," I said. "That's some bedside manner."

"I'm not a doctor," he replied. "And you came looking for me."

"I did not."

"Is this about your band?"

I told him about Viv and how she was dropping out because of God and how I had decided to scrap the plans. I did hold back on the information about my mom. I knew I couldn't leave until I told him, though.

He asked me, "And the part where your mom is melting down about something? The reason I shouldn't call her?"

You could say that I tried very hard to undersell it. "You see, I had e-mailed my father and he was coming to the show. My father contacted my mom before I could tell her. So I had opened a big honking can of worms that I couldn't put back."

He nodded and ate his fish and chips, as if that helped him think better.

Finally he said, "That wouldn't really work out so well. Her seeing him at Coachella."

"I don't see why not."

"Well, you wouldn't."

"So tell me."

"I can't tell you, Blanche. It's a complicated thing between adults. A short answer is that they have all this history. They never had a clean break and there are all these emotions not yet tied up. He wouldn't handle it so well, either, especially if I was there."

I didn't know what to say about that. It was hard to imagine my father being intimidated by Ed the Guitar Guy. But maybe guys like Ed the Guitar Guy didn't pick up on how not intimidating they were. Maybe he was a stud in his own mind.

Then I reiterated how it didn't matter because Coachella was never going to happen. Because I'd lost my band.

He nodded.

I said, "I think it's ridiculous that my mother is jealous of my relationship with my father. She wants to deprive me of it. Isn't that something that belongs to me?"

"Technically, yes. I'm sure if she were a perfect kind of person, she'd be able to step back and let it play out. But she's not. She's somebody who thought life would turn out one way and it turned out another."

"Isn't that everybody?"

He shook his head. "Some people don't dream so hard."

"Would that be you, Ed?" I said it straight out.

"Blanche, you'd be surprised but probably."

"And is dreaming hard an affliction, something to be avoided?"

"It just depends on if you can handle it," he said. "More importantly, if it's your dream. In her case, your mom was riding on his."

"Don't you feel weird talking about my mother this way?"

"I've said it all to her. She knows. She's working on it."

"So you're fixing her?"

"No, I have my stuff. I'm just a guy from a small town in the Midwest who didn't want to die there. I got out but I took plenty of baggage with me. Nobody's fixing anybody."

I didn't ask him more. I'd gone as far as I wanted to down the road of what their relationship looked like on the inside.

"Anyway," he said, reaching for his wallet, "I don't see why you can't go to Coachella. You could find another way up there."

"Ed, it's not a transportation issue. I don't have a band."

"Sure you do."

"Okay, we don't have a singer."

"They're your songs," he said. "I don't know why you wouldn't want to sing them."

"I can't sing."

"My experience tells me there are very few people who can't sing. There are mostly people who don't."

"So you're telling me to sing?" I asked. "Do you have any idea what my mother would think about that?"

He laughed. "Well, this is a separate issue. I'm telling you that you probably can sing if you want to. You can probably do anything if you want to. The things that fall by the wayside are the things we let go. I never would have let go of my own band if I hadn't found something I liked better. I liked selling guitars better. The gravest illusion we impose on ourselves, Blanche, is that life just happens to us. But the truth is, we make choices. When you say yes to one thing, you're saying no to another. And vice versa."

"Did you ever think of being a philosophy professor instead of a guitar salesman?"

He laughed. "Everybody has a philosophy, Blanche. It just comes down to how you use it. Every time I sell someone a guitar, I know it has the potential to change their lives. The rest is up to them. I just deliver the tool. I mean, what can I say? I like selling the tool."

He walked me back to the house and told me to say hello to my mom. He'd call her the next day to make sure she was okay. He didn't say anything else.

When I went inside, my mother's bedroom door was closed and the light was off.

I lay on my bed and stared at my father's guitar until I felt like it wanted to talk, wanted something from me, and then I turned over so I wouldn't have to see its scarred face or hear its silent demands. As much as I didn't want to, I thought about what Ed had said about making choices but finally just fell asleep.

That Night I Had a Dream

I WAS BACK AT THE HOUSE NEXT DOOR TO MY PARENTS' IN Silver Lake, with the ladies who took care of me, Joss and Mimi. They were exactly as I remembered them. They always had an attitude that everything was particularly right in the universe and there was nothing to worry about. The foster kids were all there, too, and I saw their faces, one by one, all their different skin shades and expressions of concern and hope and worry and pleasure.

In the dream, I was reading to them. I taught myself to read at age four, legend has it, and so it really had happened that they would gather around me to listen to me read from various picture books. I remembered the feeling I had then, of being a kind of leader, and feeling proud that I had this special skill. I remembered wanting to share that with them and being glad that I could. *My* place, in those days, was that I could read. It mattered to me. It mattered to them.

Before this dream, I would have sworn up and down that my being special was centered around having a famous father. But it came back to me, again, that I had no sense of my father's being famous. What I realized was that in that little backyard world, I had my own fame. I liked it a lot. And I moved into the dream feeling all peaceful and excited, two warring emotions that came together perfectly, and I had a sense that this was how all of life was supposed to feel.

The discrepancy in the dream was that I was my true age, fifteen, and everyone else had stayed exactly the same. I saw the eager faces of the foster kids staring up at me and I felt like I had to stop reading and tell them that something was wrong. I had grown up. But I knew if I stopped reading, they would stop looking so happy, and I just had to keep that happy expression on their faces. The feeling that had started out as being needed, in a good way, changed into a heavy sensation of being required and demanded.

It started to thunder in the distance and I could see dark clouds gathering. This wasn't a feeling that I knew much about in life, as thunderstorms were almost as rare as blizzards in L.A., so it seemed like an event I had conjured. Something I had seen in a movie. I was excited about the thunderstorm but I was also afraid and had a vague understanding that it couldn't be real. That all these worlds had no right to converge.

Someone in the group started to cry; I was really torn about whether or not to stop reading. The thunder grew louder and all the kids became distracted and I just kept reading, trying to keep them from being afraid. After a while, the kids ran away and I was suddenly alone, reading to an empty yard. My father came out into the yard then and I smiled when I saw him and finally stopped reading. I stood and walked toward him and then he was my mother, also stopped in time, a very young version of her with short curly hair and a wide smile. I walked up to her and said, "Mom, there's no one out here. It's storming and we should go inside."

She said, "Go get them back, Blanche. The kids will listen to you."

"I don't want them to listen to me. I can read but I don't know what I'm doing."

"But they believe you do," she said.

"What difference does that make? I'm just a kid."

"You're a special kid," she said.

That was exactly like something my mother would say, that infuriating dreaminess where life was a story you were telling yourself. And suddenly I was really angry and I started yelling at her. "There has to be some way to be, something that you just are, not something you make up about yourself. Anybody can decide they're special."

"Anybody can. Not everybody does."

She kept laughing and started twirling and the thunder got louder. I raced toward her and tried to grab her but my hands kept passing through her as if she were a ghost.

I woke up, just as light was starting to come through my window. I sat up, breathing hard, and told myself it was just a dream and it was all going to be fine.

I knew the dream had been trying to tell me something about what I needed to do. Now I knew what that was.

I had to get the band back together and go to Coachella, and how I felt about that on a rational level didn't matter anymore. It scared me to think that was what Viv would call Guidance. I didn't call it that. I called it a dream.

But as I lay there waiting for the rest of day to break, I knew it was as real as anything. I knew what I could do.

The Road to Coachella

SPRING ARRIVED. MONTHS PASSED. I WON'T BORE YOU WITH them.

All you really need to know is that I decided to sing.

I talked Ella back into the Fringers by telling her I would sing.

I talked Gigi back into the band by threatening to tell everyone we knew a few secrets about her from when she was thirteen!

The band practiced. I'd created a set list of five songs. Four of my own and one of my father's. We played them until they were committed to memory. I kept studying and going to classes and taking tests and getting As. I had to change my schedule at Peace Pizza. I saw Jeff watching me as I darted out the door after my shift.

My mother made it clear that since my father was coming

she and Ed wouldn't be joining me at the festival. She said she wished it could be otherwise, but there was no way.

Gigi's parents agreed to drive us. Her mother made T-shirts and flyers and plans for where we would stay and where we would eat. I kept e-mailing my father and he answered regularly. We would meet next to the stage where we were set to perform an hour before the event. We had the sixth slot, which meant we were going to perform at around three on the day of the Unsigned Competition. He mentioned my mother, admitting that he'd told her about his coming. She e-mailed back and said she wasn't coming. He made no comment other than that.

He wrote:

> Should I bow out gracefully? I don't want to interfere.

I answered:

> That's her own thing. You should come. I'm looking forward to seeing you.

He shot back:

> And I'm looking forward to seeing you. I just don't want to be disruptive. I remember those festivals. On the one hand, you want to be entertaining. The audience expects that. On the other hand, you want to demonstrate your art. It's a delicate balance.

I thought about what he said and replied:

> I think I have a good set list.

Two seconds later he answered:

> Don't forget about the tempo change. That's a really dynamic move. Do you know what I mean? Change makes people sit up and listen. Think about it. Everyone likes a shift in the mood, even if it's complete silence.

I wanted to ask, *Is that what you think you did by leaving? Did you change the tempo? Did you make everyone sit up and listen? It's one thing to do it for an audience, but what about your kid and wife?*

I didn't, though. I kept the conversation on the level of music.

My mother and Ed let me make my plans. They weren't involved. Ed didn't say another word about the night I'd cried. I was grateful.

Coachella was the last weekend in April, and the week before, I was feeling confident, even if I had butterflies in my stomach. Ella and Gigi had started to look at me the way the kids did in my dream. I'd explained the songs again and told them their parts, the tempo, and what I was going to say between songs. They never argued and waited for orders.

I never figured out the tempo change. We tried it a couple of times but the band wasn't ready for it. I changed the lyrics in my songs and reworked some of the chord changes and Ella and Gigi went with them.

I asked my father in an e-mail:

> Did you ever feel that too much responsibility is given to one person? And you don't want to be that much in charge?

He finally e-mailed:

> A visionary carries a lot of weight.

I said to him:

> The tempo change, it's too hard. You have to get everyone to agree with you on it.

He responded:

> Yes. That's why it's a challenge.

I worked with Mr. Carmichael after school on singing. He gave me good tips and exercises to strengthen my voice. He was nice enough never to tell me that I wasn't a good enough singer. He said, "The important thing is to sound like yourself and infuse it with meaning." One day, in between vocal workouts, he asked, "What was it like, having Duncan Kelly as a father?"

I didn't get mad at him for asking. I told him I didn't know, because I really didn't.

All the pieces of Coachella fell into place, and two nights before we left I was supposed to work at Peace Pizza. I decided to do it to calm my nerves. I was spreading out dough and pizza sauce and grated cheese in the back when Jeff appeared.

"So this is it, Street. Maybe your last few days of obscurity," he said.

"Unlikely," I said. We smiled at each other. "I'm not going to get famous. I'm just playing a lame bill at a famous festival. No one is going to come to see us."

Jeff waited for me after closing up shop. It had fallen on me to count the money in the cash register.

Jeff said, "How did we do?"

"We made a hundred and ten percent profit, which is probably wrong."

"It usually is when you do it. I like that you have us too far on the profit side. It shows an attitude of optimism."

I walked toward my mother's house and he fell into step beside me.

I said, "Why do you keep on seeing good things in me? Why can't you just see me as a freak?"

He smiled and said, "I try but I always come up short."

"I'm not a normal girl and I've noticed you like normal girls."

"How have you noticed that?"

"I've observed."

He shook his head and said, "I don't believe in normal."

"You're the only one."

"I'm not the only one."

I stopped and said, "Jeff, I'm not your kind of girl."

"I don't have a kind of girl," he argued.

"Yes, you do, whether you know it or not. You're going to go on with your life and be an engineer or whatever. I'm not in your landscape."

"What do you know about my landscape?"

"I know you have a real shot at joining the real world and I'm always going to be someone on the fringe. I'm a Fringer."

Jeff seemed to think about that for a moment and then he said, "Blanche, you're an artist."

I turned on him. "What the hell is that supposed to mean?"

He shrugged. "I don't know, exactly, except I don't have that ability but I like to be next to it."

"Oh, I'm some kind of exotic animal?"

"I don't know how you define it. But when I look at you, I always see someone who doesn't look at the world the way the rest of the people do."

"So you're admitting it. I'm a freak."

He shrugged again.

"Everybody has to be what they are. I know I'm a gear-head. It's not like I would have picked that, but it's what I am. I look at you and I see someone who has a different idea about life. People like you put into words or music ideas about life so we can understand it. You give us something bigger to dream."

"That's a nice way of saying I'm a freak."

"I don't really believe in freaks. I believe in artists and visionaries."

"I know what that means. A crazy person."

"Do you think you're a crazy person?"

We had veered off from my path toward home and were approaching the beach. The sound of the water meeting the sand was soothing. I stood very still. Jeff was staring at me.

I said, "Jeff, there are days when I wish my parents were accountants and I was following in their footsteps, when the only thing I ever knew or cared about was numbers. Just some undeniable truth. I hate how uncertain it all is."

He shook his hair and said, "Blanche, you're just full of it. I see how excited you get about the music."

"I do and then I feel crazy. I sit in my room and I dream about feeling like other people. Not looking like them or behaving like them but feeling like them. Do you understand?"

"Sort of."

"And then when I think of being that way, the way my mother is now, settling for a quiet life, I feel completely miserable. There's just all this tension all the time. I'm pulled all over the place. And the only relief from that is to write something or play something. That's how I end up doing it. It's not pleasant.

"But you," I went on, surprised at how much I was talking, "you are a different story. You have your idea of a perfect system. You see the numbers and they calm you down because they make sense."

"Numbers are mystical, too," he said. "Somebody was once crazy enough to envision geometry and algebra and calculus. They ran out of words and started talking in numbers and theories. Think of Einstein and the guys who created the computer. In a lot of ways, they stopped making sense to the people around them."

"This is different. This place where I live doesn't even make sense to me. Don't try to walk next to me. Trust me, just be where you are."

"Is this you telling me to leave you alone?" he asked.

"I don't know."

"I'd rather not but I will."

"No, just don't envy me. Or admire me. Or pity me. Or whatever that is in your eyes." I looked at him.

"I like you, Blanche. I really do."

"Well, you might want to reconsider that, too."

He leaned in and kissed me like we'd been doing it all our lives.

"Too late," he said.

SECOND SET

The Real Road to Coachella

ANYTIME YOU GET MORE THAN THIRTY MILES OUTSIDE OF LOS Angeles County, the landscape turns post-Apocalypse. It's *Mad Max* territory; *the hills have eyes*. Mostly because the world around us is a desert. L.A. is a desert, too, but they've drained the rest of the state, making it look like a regular city. Going to Coachella, we drove past barren landscapes with scraggly brush and literal tumbleweeds and trailers parked at the foot of dry red and yellow rocky hills. We drove past outlet conglomerates and car dealerships and In-N-Out Burgers. It was all so ugly.

Gigi's parents had rented a van and loaded all our equipment in the back. Ella and Gigi and I stared out the windows and we all indulged in our own thoughts while the Stones rattled on.

"Some pretty big acts are playing here," Rodney said.

"Some people I remember from my day. I'm looking forward to checking out the scene."

Gigi rolled her eyes at me and I smiled.

The plan was to play at the Unsigned Competition that day and spend the night and check out the regular festival the next day. Ordinarily I would have been excited about all the bands I'd get to see, but I couldn't think past our own performance. I didn't let myself. Because the first stop I'd have had to make was meeting my father again for the first time in almost ten years. When I started thinking about that, my brain started falling apart. The Rodney Stones had us staying in the Royal Desert Inn and Spa. This was not, as you might imagine, where the other unsigned bands were staying. The minute we walked into the lobby I realized why rich people were the way they were. My limited experiences with hotels were not like that. A clerk handed you the key and told you where the vending machines were.

Once in the room, which was practically as big as our house, Gigi started looking at all the amenities the spa had to offer and asked if we could get massages after the gig. She was more like her parents than I'd figured.

I stood at the window and looked at the cloud-shaped pool with all the beautiful tanned bodies in it and I realized there was a whole world I'd never even thought about.

"What's wrong?" Gigi said, joining me at the window. "Are you afraid of heights or something?"

"No. Why?"

"You don't have any color in your face. Are you going to faint?"

"It's all a lot," I said to her.

"But you know what you're doing. I mean, this is your thing."

I struggled to smile. Now was not the time to tell her that I didn't feel I had a thing.

Her parents came into our room and clapped their hands together like excited children.

Her mother said, "Girls, we should head over. Only an hour until sound check."

I put my hand to my heart to see if there was any chance of my dropping dead right that moment.

No such luck.

Coachella

It was ordinary and it was magical. It was everything and it was nothing. It was the energy of all those people coming together, throwing up their tents and lugging in food and toys and sneaking in drugs and alcohol. It felt like the most important place I'd ever been and it felt like a big dusty field in the middle of nowhere for no reason.

These were my mixed emotions as we walked into the wide-open space in the desert that was Coachella. I didn't want to think of my mother not being with me. I just wanted to think about seeing my father, at last.

There were stages everywhere, but so far from each other that you could hardly see them all at once. There were a main stage for the headliners, two slightly smaller stages for the midlevel bands and half a dozen tents for the smaller acts.

The Unsigned Competition was taking place on the main stage, where people like Rage Against the Machine and the Red Hot Chili Peppers and the Arcade Fire and Björk had played. We were going to be up there. The Fringers. Up there.

We walked past all the performance artists and the huge sculptures of abstract things and the smattering of amusement park rides and the technicians still putting the finishing touches on everything. People had already arrived and were milling around, or sitting on blankets and eating. It was only about half as full as it was going to be. That was too much to think about.

When we got to the main stage, we were greeted by concert organizers and some techs and a sound guy, and before I had time to be nervous, we were being asked all these questions about our instruments and suddenly I had to think about music. I was grateful for that.

The Clauses were just finishing up their sound check when we went in to start ours. Redmond Dwayne, who had buzzed his hair for no discernible reason, was coming off the stage with his guitar slung over his shoulder. He pretended not to know us, just gave us a kind of rock star chin wave, and that was fine with me. I was focused on getting my gear set up. Then he circled back around because, I suspected, he didn't like my nonreaction.

"Hey, Blanche, right?"

"Yeah."

"Good luck up there."

"You too."

"There are some good bands here. The dudes from Kentucky, of all places. Watch out for them."

"I will."

He looked around as if something was missing. Which, of course, it was.

"Where's the singer?" he asked.

"You're looking at her."

"Oh," he said. "Creative differences?"

"More like spiritual ones."

"Well, I'm sure you've done the right thing."

He said that like he wasn't at all sure. Which made him happy.

He said good luck again and left.

We got through sound check without anything terrible happening. At first I was so nervous, looking at all that open space and all those people staring at the stage, I could barely make a sound come out of my guitar or my mouth. But the rest of the band had a lot of energy and I just fell into the rhythm and then I was doing all the stuff I knew how to do. In the back of my mind, the whole time, was the wonder if one of those people staring at the stage was my father.

We only got to do one song for sound check so after that we went to get something to eat. I looked compulsively at my watch. I still had another hour before I was supposed to meet him. And I still hadn't told anyone what was happening. I didn't know what I was going to do in the moment, if I was going to introduce him to people or keep him a secret. The whole thing was so unimaginable. In fact, I was starting to believe I'd dreamed the whole scheme.

Ella and Gigi wanted corn on the cob, so I followed them.

We were feeling a little conspicuous since our school uniforms were still our "costumes." We'd added touches to them, scarves and chains and belts, and I'd chosen studied bed head for my hairstyle, so you could tell we were going for something, not just schoolgirls gotten lost. But the problem with going for an image was that it didn't entirely make sense out of context. Standing at the corn on the cob stand, I could feel festivalgoers staring at us.

Ella said, "I can't decide if I like it or not."

"I do," Gigi responded. "Any kind of attention is good attention, right?"

"To a neurotic personality," I said.

But it was kind of cool. The stares made you feel as if you were doing something other people couldn't do. Or wouldn't do. Willingness, again. Just getting up there.

While I was holding that thought in my head, I surveyed the crowd, the people who were watchers, not yet willing to get up there, and I connected with them. I remembered when I was that person. I wondered if there was any such thing as going back, being satisfied to be someone who watched. I realized that I listened to music differently and I was looking forward to seeing all the professional acts now that I knew what it felt like to stand on a stage. I could get ideas about moves and arrangements. The universe felt like a classroom to me now, in a school where I was interested in all the subjects and I wouldn't get a grade.

When my eyes landed on him it was so sudden, I couldn't look away.

I was sure I was conjuring my father. This wasn't the moment, after all. The moment was still a half an hour away, by the stage.

But he was standing there, a few feet away from the veggie wraps stand. My famous father eating one and looking at nothing in particular.

He was skinnier than I remembered and older. But other than that, it was as if I'd just seen him the day before. I suddenly recalled everything about him. His stance, the way he bent one knee and kept one hand in a back pocket and he tilted his head and moved it around when he looked at the world, as if guarding against an attack or expecting some delightful surprise. Either one would be material for him.

I could hardly breathe. The sounds of the festival retreated. I was aware of Ella and Gigi chattering but I had stopped hearing the words. I wanted to run away because this was not how it was supposed to happen. It was supposed to be a slow-motion walk toward each other and a soulful embrace and some tears. My tears, I guess. Sometimes I saw him picking me up and twirling me around like when I was little. But it wasn't supposed to happen with him eating a veggie wrap and me holding an ear of corn.

I was seriously considering walking away when his eyes landed on me.

His mouth drew a straight line. And then he waved. Just that. A wave.

I dropped my ear of corn into a barrel and walked toward him.

As I got closer his smile got bigger and he turned his

head from side to side as if deciding whether or not all my parts were there, whether he wanted to purchase me and take me home.

Maybe. It's possible that was just me.

"Well," he said. "Here you are."

"It's me."

He shook his head. "I'm taking it all in."

He was so much smaller than I remembered. Only a few inches taller than me. To be fair, I was tall for my age, but all I could ever remember was looking up at him. Knowing that if he was going to pick me up or meet my gaze directly, he'd have to bend. Watching him lower himself to be on equal terms, feeling him elevate me, that was the whole idea of having a father. And now it felt as if we were standing practically nose to nose, and I didn't know what to make of it. I felt like crying and then I pushed that feeling back and searched for another one. I settled on relief. He was here. He hadn't let me down.

His eyes were still a shocking black. That was how my mother described them. It was a shock to stare into them; it was almost a worry. They were so dark you were afraid you were going to fall in or see your own reflection.

But the truth, she said, was you weren't even going to see half of what was there.

He took another bite of veggie wrap and threw it away. Then he continued to stare at me.

His dark hair was a lot grayer and a little spiky. His skin was tanned and starting to leather. He still had all his earrings—you stopped counting at seven. His lips were as red as if he were wearing lipstick. I could see how handsome he used to be. I could see that man still in him but I wasn't sure anyone else ever could.

He opened his arms and I fell into them and my knees buckled a little. I yelled at them in my mind and then I was standing a little too straight, feeling like a rock against his James Dean–style Windbreaker.

"How . . . how is it?" I asked when he finally let go.

"How's what?"

"Being back in the world."

He laughed. "Oh, I recognized it right away. I fell right into its customs. It's not so bad." He gestured around him. "This is something. We never had anything like it in my day. Nobody went to see festivals back then. Arena shows. That was it."

"I guess it's a throwback to the sixties."

"Sure. All this camaraderie in the open air. Someone could start a revolution."

He smiled and rubbed a knuckle across my cheek. "I can't believe you."

"Why?"

"You're grown. You look like your mother. You got the red hair."

"Well, it's dyed a little. It's less red on its own."

He just smiled, staring at me.

Then he said, "Is she here?"

"No. She couldn't . . . she was busy . . . she had to work."

He nodded. "I didn't figure she'd want to see me."

"Oh, she wanted to."

He gave me a one-armed hug. "You don't have to make things better than they are. That's not your job. Not anybody's job. Besides, I'm happy to have this time with you."

"How long are you here for?"

"Just the week. I'm driving up north to see some friends. Then it's back to Paradise."

"I wonder. I mean, if it's so great . . . I wonder if I shouldn't come over and visit you sometime?"

His face didn't change so if he hated the idea he hid it well.

He said, "Absolutely. Maybe a graduation present. When does that happen?"

"Two more years."

"Well, maybe before that. But let's not jump ahead. We've got today."

"Yeah, and maybe you could stay for the concerts tomorrow?"

"Maybe."

By now Ella and Gigi had figured out what was going on. They wandered over, keeping a bit of a distance, until I waved them over, indicating it was safe.

"Ella, Gigi, Dad. Duncan Kelly."

They mumbled something about being honored and shook his hand.

"So this is the band? Nice look. The Fringers. I get it." He pointed to Ella. "Drummer?"

She nodded.

"Bass?" he questioned Gigi.

"Yes, but it's not my first instrument. I'm a pianist. But we needed bass and my dad used to play so I just picked it up in a matter of weeks."

I widened my eyes at her. She was turning into her own PR agent, as if she were auditioning for him. When she saw my expression she just shrugged.

"Well, congratulations on getting here," he said. "I'm looking forward to seeing you."

I saw Rodney and Erica approaching and my stomach started to turn over. I realized it was getting close to time to start and that this was it for my big encounter with my father. We could talk later but the grand reunion moment was complete. It wasn't what I'd thought it would be. Nothing is. But it was good. And now he could see me play and that would seal the deal. He would know what he had started, he would know what he had walked away from, and I doubted he'd let so much distance exist between us again.

"Time to get ready," Rodney shouted. "Got to tune up and everything."

I winced and so did Gigi. She turned to my father.

"He doesn't really know about music."

Dad just smiled. "He's right. You can't tune too much."

"Okay, let's go," I said.

Dad lingered. He said, "I'll be over in a minute. I just want to take in the surroundings."

We walked away and I glanced once over my shoulder. I saw him watching the crowd and I wondered what was going through his head. I wondered if he was remembering his time in the spotlight. I saw someone turning to look at him and I felt like he was aware of it. Then I had a terrible feeling in my stomach. Maybe he was waiting to be recognized.

I put that thought away and moved on toward the empty stage.

The Show Goes On

When we took the stage, I felt all the things you feel times a hundred. I felt important because people were staring at me and I felt like a fraud because I couldn't pull it off and I felt proud because somewhere I believed I could. Of course, I remembered my father said that every time he took the stage he told himself, "I'm up here and you're not." He said the willingness to get up there absolved you of anything that could go wrong.

I told my mother that once, and I remember this amused look passing across her face.

"You don't agree?" I asked her.

"I don't know. I've never gotten onstage. I only know that he tortures himself when it doesn't go well. So I'm not sure how much he knows about absolution."

I remembered what she said even though I didn't completely understand what absolution was. Or self-torture for that matter. I knew plenty about it later but back then I couldn't imagine beating myself up when it felt like you had the whole world to do that for you if you wanted it.

Still, I tried to hold on to that idea when I got on the stage and started plugging my guitar in and making sure I had capos and picks and the set list on the floor in front of me. The sound guy kept coming out to make sure everything was plugged in and to test our levels. "Is that enough guitar for you?" he'd ask, referring to the monitor. As if all of this were about pleasing me. As if I were the star.

Every time I looked straight ahead, I saw all these people and this vast open space and I realized that I was actually at Coachella. That made me feel like I was in some kind of dream. Or, for a very brief moment, I had an understanding that I had envisioned this and I had somehow made it happen. Including the part where I brought my father into the dream. And if that could be true for Coachella, it could possibly be true for the rest of my life.

Maybe like Ella said: What's the difference between hoping for the best and praying?

I searched the crowd for him but couldn't see him. I decided not to worry about it. It wasn't likely he had flown all the way from Hawaii to miss the set. I did, however, see Redmond Dwayne, standing in front of the stage, smiling at me. I wondered what that expression on his face meant. Was it just a really bad disguise? I had already caught him hoping for my failure. It was only fair because I was hoping for his, too. There seemed to be something else in it, too. A twinkle. Like warriors before a match. Knowing they had finally found worthy opponents.

I smiled at him. He smiled back.

My heart flopped around in my chest.

Gigi touched me on the arm and I jumped a little.

"Hey, is this really the time for that?"

"No. You're right. I'm not even interested in him. Do you need a set list?"

"No, I have it, but the stage manager wants to talk to you."

"Where?"

"Backstage."

I went down the stairs and behind the curtain and saw a woman with a headset and a clipboard. I was surprised to see her talking to my father.

I went over to them.

She gave me a big grin and said, "You're Blanche? Honestly, we had no idea."

"No idea what? Who are you?"

She giggled nervously. I could tell my dad was the cause of that.

"Sorry, I'm Meg, the stage manager, and I just found out that your dad is, well, your dad."

My father looked at me and smiled and shrugged.

"So I was talking to Paul, the producer of this segment, and he thought it would be a great idea for your dad to join you onstage."

"You mean at the end?"

"The end, the beginning, wherever you want to work him in."

I looked at her. I didn't look at him.

"Oh. Well. Is that appropriate? This is the Unsigned Competition."

Dad laughed. "I don't have a label."

"But you wouldn't want to do that."

I couldn't bring myself to say these words: *Because this is my show.*

Somehow the silence said that anyway.

"Whatever you're comfortable with, Blanche," he said.

I felt myself falling through space. Everything went out of focus for a moment and came back in. I looked at Meg and my father and I couldn't imagine how I'd gotten here from where I'd been just a second before.

Meg said, "I see on your set list that you're doing 'Glass Half Shattered,' which is your dad's song." She turned to my father. "I love that song, by the way."

"Thanks," he said.

"Anyway, I see you're closing with it, too, so why don't we just have him come on right before that song?"

I looked at Dad. He was smiling at me in a way that I couldn't interpret. Way more mysteriously than the way Redmond Dwayne was looking at me. I couldn't tell if it was affection or pride. Maybe some of that was in there. But I saw a glint of something that worried me. He raised his chin a little, and in that gesture was the tiniest question and the question was, *Please?*

Persuasion.

He needed this. He was asking me for it.

Now my stomach felt really bad, churning around as if I'd swallowed a sudden poison.

This was my father. My sainted father. The artist. The dreamer. The philosopher, the visionary.

Please.

"Okay," I said without much emotion.

Because it didn't matter much anymore.

Nothing mattered much anymore.

As easy as I'd thought my life was going to be just a few seconds before, that's how hard I suddenly knew it was going to be now and for a long, long time.

We played as well as we ever had. Better. I'd say flawlessly except for a couple of bad notes Gigi hit on the bass because she was busy trying to find Redmond Dwayne in the audience, which might have been his evil plan by standing there.

Then, before my dad made his entrance onto the stage, Meg came out and made a big deal about him. She announced half his credits and called him the Vanguard of Poetic Punk, or something equally disturbing, and it suddenly occurred to me that I used to say things like that. Back when I was a critic. Back when I was somebody who just talked about other people's work in a sassy way, trying to invent new phrases and make it all sound so important. That was before I knew what it was like to try to put the whole thing together and actually perform for people and get something across to them.

My dad walked out with shy posture, waving one hand

to the crowd and carrying a guitar with the other. He had brought his own guitar. I was floored. Now I knew this idea had occurred to him a while ago.

The crowd went nuts.

Gigi and Ella stared at me. All I could do was shrug.

I saw Mr. and Mrs. Stone in the audience, clapping and whistling.

I saw Redmond Dwayne clapping as hard as he could and staring at my father as if they might make eye contact and become friends.

When I looked back at Gigi and Ella, I found they had gotten into it now and had somehow started to believe the applause was for them, too. They were smiling and waving at the crowd.

My father strapped on his guitar. He approached the mike and said, "Test, one, two," into it and the crowd went nuts again, as if he'd actually done something.

He smiled at me and then said into the mike, "It's been a long time since I've done this."

More rapturous screaming.

He said, "I want to thank my daughter, Blanche, for talking me out of hiding."

Again with the roar of approval.

He said, "It's an honor and privilege to play with the Founders."

"Fringers," I said, off-mike. He'd said it right just a while ago.

"What?" he asked with his face.

"We're the Fringers," I repeated.

"Oh, right, the Fringers," he said into the mike.

People laughed.

I turned so hot I thought I might blow a circuit in the amp. It was a wonder my guitar didn't feed back from the electricity in my body. I thought for just a second of putting my guitar down and walking offstage.

Sometimes I still wake up in the middle of the night wondering why I didn't do that.

It would have been something I could have owned. I could have taken the whole thing and made it into my moment, which was the original idea.

But I just kept thinking about the advice my father, the one I'd adored, had given me as a little girl and all my life. No matter what happens, he said, play through.

So we played through.

Later, one of the music critics from some national magazine said in print, "Duncan Kelly might have had a more shining moment onstage, or a more brilliant rendition of 'Glass Half Shattered,' but I can't find anyone to attest to it."

The thing the rock critic never mentioned was that the particular arrangement of "Glass Half Shattered" was mine—Blanche Kelly's. In front of the crowd, my father even found himself adjusting to some of the changes I made onstage. He wasn't used to the song having drums, for example, and I had made up a guitar-picking pattern that threw him at first, but he fell into step with it. The song he was so famous for was just him and an acoustic guitar and some violins added later. The song was all about him. And this time, he had to incorporate all these other sounds and people into it. What he figured out, halfway through the song, was that the band was not there to fight the song but to support it. And I saw him relax into it and finally he rode along on it and even as his voice lifted above all of us, I knew that the platform he'd found to fly from had been provided by us. I'd gotten him there; I was elevating him. And then it hit me. That was what I'd always done.

But I don't want to take everything away from him. Listening to him sing the song he wrote, all those years ago, and hearing the cry in his voice and watching the way he melted into the whole expression as if nothing else on earth mattered, I saw his greatness. I understood why everyone loved him. I saw why my mother had put everything in her life on hold for him and I saw why he found it so hard to live in the world with the rest of us. He was blessed or cursed with whatever that was. The vision. The voice. The need to bring something down from the metaphysical and make people believe they could live it. I saw his dream and I saw his isolation and I felt all the pain he must have felt for so many years when he was trying to just dwell among the mortals.

I saw it all. I just didn't care.

Beer Garden

Coachella Jail isn't really a jail. It's the back room of a security office toward the end of the field, behind the tents and the barbecue and the performance art and all. You can't really see it from your blanket when you're enjoying the festivities. I guess that's because they don't want you thinking about malfeasance while you're eating your frozen lemonade. It's a festival, after all, and even though people like to think of themselves as outlaws and renegades, they don't necessarily want to be reminded of the experience.

I was sitting in the back room of the Coachella Jail drinking a bottle of water and rubbing my head and wishing the real drunks in the room could tone it down a notch or two. I hadn't really tied one on. I was such a lightweight that the two beers I downed in a minute after I'd snuck into the beer garden had gone right to my head. Then someone passed around a joint and I took a hit of that, even though I had no idea what I was doing and coughed more than I inhaled. But I started feeling like I had gone to all that trouble to sneak into the beer garden and I had gotten some guy I barely knew to buy me a beer and I had consumed most of it in one enthusiastic swallow, so I was obligated to act a little cheerful about it.

I was getting a lot of attention in the beer garden because I had a guitar with me, in a gig bag, on my back, which made me look completely professional and legit, and the crying I'd done all the way off the stage and to the beer garden had made my makeup run and I was Courtney Love heroin chic.

The saddest thing was that nobody noticed me leaving after the performance, particularly my father. When I drifted from the backstage area, I could still hear everyone talking about how great the performance was. Redmond Dwayne had come up and was saying nonsense to my dad about what a genius he was, what a seminal artist. Gigi was giggling and telling Redmond how blown away she was by the whole thing and even Ella kept saying, "Awesome." Mr. and Mrs. Stone joined in and then some reporters swarmed over. I grabbed my guitar and quietly took off.

I didn't know where I was going. I didn't know there was anything called a beer garden until I got right up to it. I noticed that people were showing wristbands to get in and I just piled in behind them and they never thought to ask me because I had the heroin eyes and the guitar.

I figured it wouldn't be long till my friends or my father started looking for me so I should probably hammer back the first beer. I made friends with a bunch of people from Orange County and they started talking about all the headliners they were excited about seeing and this was their third year at Coachella and every time it got better and so on.

"You guys just see the Unsigned thing?" somebody in the group asked.

The others said no.

"I didn't, either, but I hear this guy Duncan Kelly showed up," said this dude in a backward baseball cap and a white T-shirt.

"Wasn't he from the nineties? Some big guy from back then?" asked a girl in tight, short animal print.

"Yeah," said Baseball Cap. "He was seminal."

I started laughing and the baseball cap guy bought me another beer for no reason and finally it occurred to someone to ask me why I had a guitar. I told them I was an artist and that I was playing later and they tried to get me to tell them which big band I was part of but I wouldn't. From that point on they just kept buying me beer. But like I said, after the second one I was pretty cooked so I kept spilling them or pouring them out.

I wasn't disappointed when the security guards pulled up. I guess the guitar and the costume were the dead giveaway in terms of who I was.

I was already standing before the bald guy in the blue uniform started over and barked, "Blanche Kelly?"

"That's me."

He repeated my name and said, "Do you realize you are breaking the law by being in here?"

"I guess."

"Your party tells us you're not over the age of twenty-one. Therefore it's illegal for you to be in the beer garden."

"Which party? This party?" I said, gesturing to my new friends. "They would never say that about me."

"Have you been consuming alcohol?"

"You know what, Brad," I said, randomly naming him, "why don't we just skip this part and you take me wherever you're going to take me?"

He took the handcuffs out and turned me around but the other security guard said, "Hey, no, don't do that. She's a kid."

"She's a drunken kid."

"Come on. Let's just take her in and they'll come get her."

"It's protocol," Brad said.

"Look," said the other guy, lowering his voice, "it's Duncan Kelly's kid."

Amazing how that name, even when said at the lowest volume, caused people to perk up.

I offered my hands defiantly. "Cuff me."

"Just get in the cart."

"No, I insist. Cuff me. It's protocol!"

Once I started yelling he kind of had to cuff me, so I let them lead me off to the security cart, and behind me I heard the Orange County people say, "Did you hear that? It's Duncan Kelly's kid."

"No way," another said.

As we were riding slowly through the open field, moving in and out of clumps of festivalgoers, one of the security guards, not Brad, said, "How does that feel?"

"How does what feel?" I asked.

"Being famous."

"I'm not famous. He is."

"It always looked awful to me, being famous," he said. "That's why I avoided it."

The worst thing that happened to me in Coachella Jail was that even though there were only about six of us in there, the person nearest to me threw up. It was a girl and she looked about my age. What was her problem?

I looked across the room and saw a guy somewhere in his twenties with nothing obvious wrong with him staring at me as if he was wondering what my problem was. He seemed completely sober and there wasn't a mark on him so I figured he must have been a drug dealer or something. Then I saw that his hand was taped up.

"Hit somebody?" I asked.

He laughed, an embarrassed laugh. "Yeah."

"Somebody important?"

"I don't know. I didn't know him."

"Was it worth it?"

He thought about it, pulling at his lip. "So far."

I laughed.

"What happened to you?" he asked.

"I drank some beer. I'm underage."

"Kinda harsh, keeping you in here."

"Yeah."

"What's the ax for?"

I realized he meant my guitar.

"I didn't know anybody had an ax since Jimi Hendrix."

"No, it's back now. The terminology. You play?"

"Yeah."

"You in the show?"

"Me? I'm just a kid."

He slowly pointed a finger at me. "Wait, I saw you. You were in the Fringers."

I looked away. Something about him saying that made me want to cry. He even knew the band's real name.

"Yeah, I guess I was."

"I saw your act. You guys were great. Are you the singer?"

"Singer, guitar player, that's me."

"It's great, it's kind of punk Beatles but with some Replacements or something?"

"The Replacements are punk Beatles."

"Yeah, but different still. And the girl thing completely works. I don't mean to insult you but it's a great twist."

"Thanks."

"Were those your songs?"

"Yeah, I wrote them."

"Cool. I'm Jeremy."

"Hi, Jeremy. I'm Blanche."

"Blanche, you have an awesome voice, too."

"Right."

"No, seriously. I wasn't even drinking when I saw you guys. I mean, I don't drink, to be honest. I probably should, it would keep me from getting in fights with guys who drink too much at festivals."

"Yeah. That's funny."

"And then, who was that dude who got up there with you? Everyone was going nuts."

I didn't answer. I just stared at the ground.

He nudged me. "I'm just teasing. I know who he is."

"Great."

He said, "You guys were just awesome even before he got up there."

"Jeremy, if you are trying to cheer me up, you're doing a hell of a job."

"A lot of respectable musicians have famous fathers. And mothers."

"That'll do. You can go back to being quiet now."

"Can I get on your mailing list?"

"I don't think there's going to be a mailing list. I think that was our first and last performance."

"No, don't say that. Here."

He stood up and reached into his back pocket with his good hand and gave me a card. It said MIGHTY MIGHTY MUSIC PRODUCTIONS. JEREMY WILKINS, PRESIDENT.

"What is this?" I said. "Something you have made up to impress girls at parties?"

"No, I'm in college. That kind of thing doesn't work in college."

"Where do you go?"

"UC Santa Barbara."

"What do you produce at Mighty Mighty Music Productions?"

"Nothing yet. I mean, my own stuff. But I'm looking to branch out. Hey, can't hurt to stay in touch."

"Wouldn't that be a great story. How did you get your start, Blanche? Well, we met in Coachella Jail."

He laughed. "Sounds good to me."

I knew I was never going to see Jeremy Wilkins again because he was that much older than me and he had a tweed cap on and I couldn't imagine myself knowing a guy like that. But there was something warm and sincere in his eyes, like someone I remembered from a long time ago. Something about his eyes made me believe in connection. I saw that people on the same course in life somehow managed to find each other, if only for a moment.

He smiled at me.

And then it sounded like fifteen people were storming Coachella Jail when Gigi, Ella and the parents came in wanting to know where I was and if I was all right.

"Your fan club is here," Jeremy said.

"Actually," I said, "I think you're it."

The Rodney Stones drove Gigi and Ella back to the hotel and my father and I followed in his rented car. He drove it quietly, one hand on the wheel, staring intently at the road. Except to figure out that I was all right and to assure me that no charges were going to be pressed, the adults didn't have anything to say to me.

Gigi and Ella both gave me questioning glances before heading upstairs. I wanted to tell them what was going on but I didn't know.

"I guess we're going to call it a night, then," Rodney Stone said.

"Yes, we're all exhausted," Erica added.

They were the kind of parents who thought things

automatically got better if you didn't talk about them or if you just kept putting a cheerful spin on them.

"Are you going to stay with us or your father?" Erica asked.

I looked at my father for the answer.

He said, "I think Blanche should stay here. But we're going to hang out and talk for a while."

"That's a good idea," Rodney said cheerfully, as if this were all some big summer camp. "You have your key, Blanche?"

I showed it to him.

"Okay, then, good night. And congratulations, girls."

"On what?" I asked.

Ella and Gigi looked at each other, then at me.

"We got third place. There was a little ceremony. We accepted it on your behalf."

"Oh," I said.

"It's a check and a certificate," Gigi said.

"Five hundred bucks," Ella said. "Split three ways. That ought to pay for the gas."

"Now, don't be ridiculous, we're paying for the gas," said Erica. "You girls earned that prize."

"Who got first?" I asked.

"The Clauses, of course," Ella said.

"Well, they were good," Gigi said, her eyes full of Redmond Dwayne.

"And I guess they couldn't really give it to us," I said. "I mean, it wasn't really a fair competition."

"Of course it was," Erica said.

"No. It's supposed to be an amateur competition. And not everyone up there was an amateur."

Everyone got quiet and then the elevator dinged and Rodney said, "Well, I guess it's good night, then."

The others disappeared into the elevator and the chrome doors closed and were a mirror to me and my long-lost father standing there in the lobby of some hotel in a desert.

"Let's go out by the pool," he said.

Out by the Pool

Since it was late there was no one around. The lights in the water made rippling shadows on the walls and on our faces. My father sat on the edge of a lounge chair and clasped his hands and stared at them as if he had the mysteries and the answers inside them and to open them was to let them go.

There was a couple in the Jacuzzi at the far end, away from us, and they were drinking. They laughed sporadically and the man would say, "This is living. Now *this* is living." I'm not sure what he'd been doing up to the point that he got in the Jacuzzi but apparently it wasn't living.

My father. Legend. Seminal artist. He sat there in front of me staring at his all-important hands. On a lounge chair in Palm Desert. This was the moment I'd been dreaming of, the two of us sitting together, about to talk about it all. But

I hadn't understood what the all was and I'd had no idea that it would end up like this.

When he finally spoke he said, "Blanche, there are two kinds of musicians in the world. Generous and ungenerous. If you are an ungenerous musician, no one will want to have anything to do with you."

"Except maybe other ungenerous musicians?"

He looked up from his hands.

"Now you're going to throw sarcasm into your bag of tricks?"

"It's always been in there and it's not tricks. I think psychologists call it a defense or a coping mechanism."

He ignored that.

He said, "My point is that you obviously didn't want to share the stage with me tonight and because you didn't know how to tell me that, you had to act out. You had to show instead of telling me how you felt."

"That was my first move. But I'll tell you if you want me to."

"You invited me," he said.

"I invited you to hear me play up there," I said.

"Let me finish. If you can't share the stage with someone, particularly your father, then you have to accept that you're not a generous musician."

"And that's devastating because?"

He stared at me. "Who convinced you that this kind of thing is attractive?"

"Nobody. I don't have anyone around to convince me. See, my father left when I was six and my mother never really bounced back so I end up making a lot of my own rules."

"Oh, is that what this is about?"

"Dad, seriously?" My voice was shaking but I had nothing holding me back now. "I was prepared to let you off the hook for all that. You have no idea how much I put you on a pedestal. How willing I was to do anything to see you and have a relationship with you. I was willing to overlook anything for that. I created this band and I put the whole thing together and dragged it up a million hills because I thought it was the thing that would bring you back. We'd have something in common. Something to hold your interest. I didn't know that for sure until I saw you. But guess what? You made this whole thing about you! All I wanted was for you to stand there and look at me onstage and be proud of me for something. Then you could go back to Paradise and I could kind of breathe again. You are Duncan Kelly. You didn't need me to get you out of hiding. You could have done it anytime. Any day. Anyplace. Don't you know that?"

The dark pool eyes. The ones you might fall into. He seemed to understand their power. I hadn't gotten them from him. I had my mother's mischievous quizzical green. I used to mourn that. I used to turn my face every which way in the mirror trying to see him in it. It was there but it had never been enough there for me.

He said, "I am hearing these thoughts for the first time. How could I know?"

"Because you're a father. You're a prophet and a poet. You're supposed to know things without being told, aren't you?"

"Why couldn't you have had that dream by playing with me onstage? Why wasn't that part of the picture?"

"Because I wanted it to be mine. I wanted to create something of my own and show it to you. Is that real hard for you to understand?"

"Somewhat."

"Because it's hard for you to imagine any kind of scenario where you aren't at the center?"

He smiled. "I've left you alone too long with your mother."

"I can get mad at you all by myself. I don't need help."

He stood and said, "I think we've gone as far as we can with this."

"I'd like it if you'd sit down."

"Blanche, I've seen as much as I want to."

"I didn't ask you a question. I told you what I'd like."

He kept standing. But he didn't walk away.

I said, "You can't imagine what I had to overcome to get to Coachella."

"Yes, the million hills, so you've said."

"I had to pay for everything and keep everybody from fighting and learn how to sing because my singer started getting visits from angels."

He ignored the angels.

He simply interrupted.

"I know what an ordeal it is to keep a band together, Blanche."

"Is that why you dropped out? It was too much trouble playing well with others?"

"An artist is not like other people."

"A plumber is not like other people. Everybody has a calling."

"Yes, that's right. And an artist sometimes functions best away from the calamity of ordinary life. It's oppressive having to look at the little ways and the big ways and all the ugly ways that people settle and compromise and let themselves down."

"That must have been tough for you. That must have been much more a challenge than being somebody's father."

Steady as you please, not missing a beat, he said, "I never wanted to be a father."

It took the wind right out of me. I'd been holding my own up until that point but he had dealt the fatal blow.

The thing was, I knew he wasn't just saying it to be mean. It was true.

What's more, it was the truth I had been trying to get to all the time. This was my worst nightmare realized, which, like the greatest dream, is something most people don't have to confront at my age. At any age, possibly. It's like the monster under your bed. You keep saying it's not real but sooner or later you might have to crawl under there to make sure.

I suddenly felt tired and overwhelmed so I stood up. I said, "Well, I guess we've gotten to the heart of the matter so we might as well say good night."

My father stood very still. Because the light was so distorted out there by the pool, he looked like some kind of otherworldly being, this skinny, slight man whose mannerisms were younger than his years, but whose appearance otherwise was exactly his age. He was Rock Star Forever meets Middle-Aged Guy with Burned Bridges.

His long hair swept into his face. It would have been

gray but I could see in this light that he dyed it. He was almost entirely a lie.

He said, "Blanche, I don't mean that I didn't want you."

"In vino veritas," I said.

"I'm not drinking."

"Well, your first thought's your best one or something."

"Really? Is that a scientific fact?"

"Let's look at it this way. Either you meant it, or it was something you created in the moment just to get a reaction from me. Either way, it changes my idea of you."

"Well, while we're being brutally honest, all you really have is an idea of me."

"And whose fault is that?"

"I suppose it's mine," he said, "if you insist on breaking life down into faults and blame."

"You know what, Dad? I'm just tired of thinking about it and talking about it. My head hurts. I just want to go to bed."

He said, "No, let me explain. I never wanted to be a father and then I became one. I was happy to be one but I didn't really know how. Did it ever occur to you that I took myself out of the equation because of all the damage I was doing? I saw myself inflicting it. I couldn't stop it somehow. But I needed to. So I left."

"And you never thought about what that did to us?"

"Of course I thought about it. But we all have stories, Blanche. This is mine. Yours is yours. I can't rewrite it. I can't make it different for you. First you exalted me. There was nothing I could do but destroy myself in your eyes."

"I suppose that's why you came."

"I came because you asked me to. And I thought it was time."

"And you missed your audience."

"No."

"My mother has had to do a thousand undignified jobs just to keep us in the game. She wanted the best for me. She figured out how to get me into this lame private school on scholarship. We didn't have the option of shooting for the stars, Dad. We only had the option of shooting for the best we could do. She works in a clothing store and I work in a pizza joint. Everything we do on top of that is fought for. We didn't need you to be a big rock star. We just needed you to join the fight. You didn't. We're alone."

"She has a boyfriend now. You're not so alone."

"Okay, she's got a boyfriend. After all these empty years you're going to begrudge her that?"

"You have a band."

"A band you tried to use for yourself."

"My point is, you're not alone."

"And you are? Poor you, Dad. You chose that. We had no choice. Seminal artist," I said. "What does that even mean? I can't say I know what the point is, Dad, but I'm pretty sure you've missed it."

"Look, I'm going to head back tomorrow. Let's not end it this way."

"You're not sticking around?"

"Why would I?"

"More shows, maybe?"

"Blanche, this is not an argument worth hanging on to."

"I'll be the judge of that."

I walked toward the hotel.

Behind me he said, "I'm sorry I messed everything up."

I stood with my hand on the door. I wanted to just walk through it but that comment turned me around. I didn't want it to be the last word between us.

"When?" I asked. "Today or my whole life?"

The question didn't seem to faze him. As with anything he didn't want to confront, he ignored it.

"I'd like to stay in touch," he said.

"I'll leave that up to you," I said, and put my hand on the door again.

He said, "Blanche, can you at least give me this? You might have gotten some of your talent from me."

I hated to admit it but I wanted to hear more about my talent. So I waited.

He said, "Do you realize how good you are?"

"Of course I don't," I said.

"Well, you are. If you hadn't disappeared after the set, I was going to tell you all that. How good your playing is, how much I liked your arrangement. Your singing."

It felt like a bone he was throwing me but I wasn't strong enough to give it back.

"At the very least, maybe it was that I left my guitar lying around the house. Or that you somehow turned me into your audience all this time. If I'd been around, I might have eclipsed you. But with me gone, you had all that time to dream," he said.

"Is that what you're going to tell yourself?"

"I might."

"Well, as John Lennon said, whatever gets you through the night."

"That goes for both of us, don't you think?"

"I don't know anymore."

He said, "Just consider it."

I turned and stared hard at him. Because I felt all churned up and I had a thousand things I wanted to say and I was afraid I'd never see him again.

I said, "What were you thinking? Leaving us? Did you really believe that you could just subtract yourself from the equation?"

His face looked deflated.

He said, "Yes, I really did believe that."

"You didn't think you'd leave something behind?"

"What?" he demanded. "What did I leave behind?"

"Art," I said to him. "Like blood on the walls."

"Art," he said quietly.

"And my desire to create it. You have to answer for that."

He shook his head, staring at the ground.

"No," he said. "I'm afraid you do. Because you now realize how much it matters."

"More than anything?"

"Almost. But only almost."

I did give him a smile like a benediction before I opened the door and went into the lobby of the hotel, which suddenly felt like the portal to my new life. Whatever it was going to be.

Another Guitar

THE WEDDING WAS ON THE BEACH. OF COURSE IT WAS. THE beach at sunset. That was so very my mother. She wore a white silk dress and carried violets and he wore a white silk suit but neither one of them wore shoes.

She invited Louise, and Ed got his best friend, Chuck, who was also his guitar repair guy, to perform the ceremony on the authority of the certification he had gotten out of the back of a magazine. Those things are valid and legal. I'm not making this up.

They waited until May so the weather would be nice but they somehow couldn't wait until late June when my exams would have been over and I wouldn't have been feeling so stressed out.

When I asked them why they weren't waiting for summer,

Mom said, "Well, Blanche, I expected you to put up a fight against the whole idea. I just made my plans without your permission."

"I don't know why you'd think that."

"I realize you got used to Ed but that didn't mean you'd want him as a stepfather. I thought you'd be disgusted by the thought of a wedding."

"Ed's all right. I don't object."

"I know how you revere your father."

I hadn't told her what had happened. I wasn't entirely sure I was ever going to. She hadn't asked when I got back from Coachella, even though my father's presence there had been all over the news and the Internet. Including clips of us playing together onstage. I realized that she must know, but a long time ago, my mother had made a deal with herself to limit her discussion of him. She was proud of my band, though. She had her new life. She was moving on.

I had actually gotten e-mail and fan letters about Coachella. I gave a separate interview to the *L.A. Times* that was buried in the corner of the "Calendar" section in a little box, with a headline like "The Next Generation of Visionary." It had a big picture of my father, a postage-stamp-sized one of me, and a quote from me saying, "I don't know if music is in the blood. It just feels like it's in my head."

I had said more than that but I didn't worry about it.

LaHa gave us a big reception and a lot of fanfare after Coachella. Gigi and Ella and I were on the front page of the *Manifesto*, all decked out in our uniform costumes, with full-on rock-and-roll makeup and standing by our instruments. Edgy schoolgirls. Not what you'd expect. When you looked at that picture, it seemed we'd all been together for a long time and were going great places.

The truth was, the Fringers broke up right after Coachella. On the way back home, in the car, to be honest. I was still reeling from my encounter with my father so I was sitting in the backseat just staring out the window, trying to get my breath and a picture in my head of how my life could possibly look after this. How it was going to make sense, how I was going to know what to aim for or dream about, and the only thing that kept me centered in that whole picture was the Fringers. We were together. We were good. We could come back to Coachella and win next time.

That was when Gigi said, "Blanche, I'm really glad you made us do this. It was fun."

"Yeah," Ella said, "I would have had a totally dull sophomore year without it."

I said, "You're welcome, but come on, guys. It's not like our work is done. I think we need to kick the rehearsals up to twice a week and think about finding an additional guitar player. I think an electric sound would really add a lot."

I saw Gigi exchange a glance with her parents and then look back at me.

"Blanche, I can't keep doing this. I've got to get my class president campaign together. I mean, besides studying and prepping for SATs."

"You're kidding, right?" I said.

Erica smiled at me from the front seat. "Gigi has other plans but this has been great for her, Blanche. I'm sure you'll go on to do wonderful things with your music."

I looked at Ella. She said, "I'm getting a better job this summer and I'm training for crew."

"For what?"

"Rowing. I'm going to do that next year."

"Rowing? Who are you people?"

"We want to get into good colleges, Blanche. Who are you?" Gigi said with a distinct edge.

I didn't answer her.

Without the Fringers and without my father, I had no idea who I was.

They consented to be in the Fringers long enough for that photo and article in the *Manifesto*, though, and that was nice of them. Dr. Bonny announced our success at the spring assembly and we went up onstage and took bows and everyone stared at us as if we had done something magical. They had no idea that we were just a blip on the radar and we were about to go back to the obscurity from which we'd come.

While we were up there taking our bows, I saw Viv in the audience. She was smiling and clapping and whistling through her fingers as if this were the greatest display of anything she'd ever seen. She was a fan of the Fringers. As if she'd never been one of us. I wondered about that happy, exuberant expression, totally devoid of any jealousy and resentment—so unlike what you see on the faces of teenagers normally—and I wondered how she could possibly be that way.

I supposed that seeing an angel had reminded her of who she was in the universe. It gave her a sense of purpose. I smiled at her and she smiled back and even though I wanted to be angry, something about her made me feel like it was going to be okay. Maybe not soon but eventually. As if that might be the natural order of the universe. Things being basically okay.

Two days after the wedding on the beach, while I was still studying for exams, Ed the Guitar Guy officially moved into the house, and I barely noticed. He was there all the time anyway and he had hardly any belongings to his name. I noticed that some kind of weird tribal mask went up on the living room wall next to my mother's crystals and goddesses and whatnot. And suddenly there was a black leather chair that reclined in the corner and there was a bowl of jelly beans always on the coffee table because Ed the Guitar Guy liked them and that was about it. Life went on the way it did before. Me in my room and my mom darting in and out from work and occasionally going out for coffee or tea, but when she did that, it was with Ed the Guitar Guy now instead of Louise. And when they came home they were always laughing and talking in quiet voices, like they had a secret, and sometimes they curled up on the couch and watched shows on television and laughed some more. It looked like the world's most boring life and it wasn't one I remotely wanted and somehow, I just didn't mind it at all.

One night Ed knocked on my bedroom door and asked if I wanted to talk and I said what about and he said he noticed that I hadn't been playing my guitar much since Coachella.

I told him about the Fringers breaking up. He said he

was sorry to hear it but there was no reason for me not to continue playing.

I told him I was probably going to try out for the school play or do something like that next year and that would take up a lot of my time.

"Well, there's a reason I ask," he said. He reached for something outside my door and the next thing I knew, he was handing me a guitar case. I opened it up. It was a beautiful Gibson guitar, completely intact, no hole in the body.

He said, "We got it in the store. We haven't been able to move it. I don't know why. Probably because it's discontinued, not one of their more popular models, not very flashy, but the sound is perfectly nice. And it's a small body, I thought you might like that."

I stared at it. I wanted to touch it but I was afraid to. I was afraid of how much I'd want it if I did. And I was afraid I'd be letting all that craziness back in my life.

I said, "You don't have to bribe me, Ed. You're my stepfather now and there's nothing I can do about it. I'm not bugged anyway. It's fine."

He smiled. "It's a gift, Blanche. You earned it. That was a lot of hard work, putting the band together and taking it as far as you did."

"I guess," I said, not looking at him or the guitar.

"And whatever happened up there with your father . . ."

"Nothing. Nothing happened."

"Well, I just wondered if the reason you hadn't been playing was that the guitar belonged to him."

"No, that's not it."

"And even if that's not it, a girl should have her own

guitar. They keep their vibrations, you know. The person who held it and made things happen on it or to it, those impressions stay. So this one, it's a clean slate. It's never been anybody's. But yours. If you want it."

I didn't say anything.

He stood and smiled at me. "How about I leave it here and you see whether or not you can make friends with it?"

"Fine," I said.

He touched me lightly on the shoulder and left.

The guitar sat in its red velvet, staring up at me, like a homeless pet.

I stroked its face and closed the case and decided to think about it later.

The Prayer

PEACE PIZZA. IT BECAME MY REFUGE. I GOT BACK ON MY REGULAR schedule, the one I had abandoned during the craziness of the Fringers.

I suddenly understood the name of the place. Maybe Toby had understood that when he started the business. He was a guy who just wanted to surf and hang out and he couldn't handle ambition so he started a pizza joint and that was his peace. I always thought it was some kind of political movement but maybe not. Before, I had always looked at him as someone who had given up on life. But now that I had seen my father in action, I understood people like Toby and Ed. They weren't burdened with all that want.

I thought maybe I could go with that idea. I could just make pizzas and not worry about who I was in the world. Pizza making was something some people did so they could get on with their real approach to living, which was being on some kind of board, surf or skate. It was all leading to exactly where it was.

Not so with Jeff. He had been promoted to night manager but he was going to leave in July so he could start an internship with some engineering company, which was all part of his gearhead plans. He was excited about it. He hoped the internship would help him get his scholarship to MIT. After which he had even more big plans for himself.

One night while I was mixing up sauce, Jeff came and stood beside me and said, "I didn't think you wanted me up at Coachella, so I didn't go. What's going on with your band?"

Of course, he didn't know. I hadn't shared anything with him in a long time.

"I don't have a band, Jeff. I'm just a girl who works in a pizza place."

"Hey, listen," he said. "I have an idea. Why don't I record your stuff for you?"

"What?"

"I taught myself Pro Tools on the computer. I could record you. It's pretty easy."

"I don't have a band."

"You don't need one. I can program any sound you want. I just need you to sing because I can't program that."

"Where would we do this exactly?"

"At my house. My basement. My mom let me set it up like a studio. But I haven't recorded anybody yet because, well, I didn't know any musicians who were any good until you became one."

"I'm not such a good musician."

"Okay, then just be a guinea pig. I want to experiment with my producing skills."

"Why?"

He shrugged. "Well, maybe that's just what I want to do with my fancy engineering degree."

I stared at him. I had never thought of Jeff as anything but a serious guy with serious thoughts on his mind.

Jeff smiled at me.

"After all, I helped you write your first song."

I looked away from him and swirled sauce onto a pizza.

"You should stick to building rockets or something. Music is a big hassle. Trying to keep a band together. Trying to keep everyone including yourself sane."

"Look, Street, I think we could make a good team."

He leaned against the counter and smiled at me. He had one of those confident smiles that made you wonder what it was all about, what secret powers he possessed that made him seem so comfortable with being in the world. He made you want to be next to it. Or he made me want to, anyway.

"Maybe," I said.

"Great!"

He grabbed me and lifted me up and twirled me around. I couldn't stop laughing.

"Have you completely lost your mind?" I asked when he put me down.

"Hanging on by a thread," he said, winking at me.

* * *

When I got home from work I went straight to my e-mail and checked it. There was nothing from my father. There was nothing from anyone except some photos from Gigi that her father had taken at Coachella. Looking at them was strange. It's always hard to look at yourself because the camera mushes you up and adds weight and crazy angles but really it's just hard to see yourself out of context—that is, the context of your own head. You just don't look the way you think you do. Suddenly you have to see yourself as other people see you. And even then you can't be sure that's how they see you. It just makes you confused because you understand that you're someone who goes out in the world and because of that, you're just exposed to all kinds of interpretations.

Even stranger is to see yourself onstage. I walked out there and asked people to look at me and listen to me and I held their attention the whole time and for what?

They only sent one photo with my father in it.

I was playing my guitar and singing into the mike with my eyes closed. My hair didn't look as bizarre as I feared. I looked like an actual rock star with the crazy outfit on and the dark makeup. I was surprised to see how easy it was to buy me as a rocker. As the bold artsy type. I looked as if I might actually have something to say.

In the photo, my father is playing the guitar and he's singing into the mike, but he doesn't have his eyes closed and he isn't staring at the audience. His head is turned sideways and he's looking at me. He's wearing this charming, coaxing smile, like he's willing me to look at him and I'm not doing it.

It's hard to tell what the expression is on his face. Maybe he is seeing himself in me. Maybe he's just putting on an act for the audience. Maybe he really is proud. What's more striking is the way I'm behaving. As if I don't want to know he's there. As if I somehow got there without him. As if that were possible at all.

Somehow I understood that it had all worked perfectly. In all its chaos, it had gone the way it had to go.

I heard the door close and my mother and Ed were laughing. I heard the TV go on and I heard Ed grinding beans to make coffee. He was heavily into grinding coffee beans and my mother was heavily into anything he did. She was into being taken care of. She was into him being there.

I picked up my cell phone and dialed. Viv answered.

"Hi," she said. "I never expected to see your name on my phone again."

"I'm sorry. I got so busy with Coachella."

"You don't need to explain. We don't have to be friends. I'm happy for you, though. I knew you could do it."

"I wanted to tell you something."

"Okay."

"Nobody ever asked me what prayer I wrote for the prayer box."

"I figured it was private."

"I guess it was but the thing is, it came true."

"You prayed to get to Coachella."

"No. I don't think I even need to tell you what it was. Just that it came true."

"Okay," she said.

"Does that mean I believe in God now or something?"

"I don't know. Does it?"

"I don't know."

We were quiet for a moment.

I wanted to say a lot more but I knew I couldn't. It was all forming in my head and it was coming together. But it had somewhere else to go.

"Okay, so I'll see you at school. Thanks for everything," I said.

"I didn't do anything."

"Yes, you did. You taught me how to sing."

"How did I do that?"

"By not singing."

"Well, maybe. But you're the person who made it happen. I wouldn't have gone near that prayer box without you. I wouldn't have had something to hold on to when I was lost without that. And you wouldn't have found the courage to find the band without me. I think that events just come together and create possibilities. But possibilities go nowhere without the people who recognize them. You know?"

"I sort of know. I kind of get it now."

"Thanks for the call, Blanche."

We said goodbye and I lay very still on my bed for a moment.

I could see myself writing the prayer down, scribbling it very fast, not even thinking about it because I felt like it was something I thought a thousand times a day and even wished for but I had never prayed. I never got how important it was to turn it into a prayer and then into an intention. It was the difference between wishing it and living it.

I want to get to know my father.

That's what I put in the box.

Because I didn't realize that when your prayers get answered, it doesn't look the way you expect it to. It doesn't look like happiness, necessarily. It just looks like getting what you asked for.

I thought about Jeff recording my songs in his basement. I remembered how he said he was hanging by a thread. I pictured us collaborating and coming up with great ideas. I saw us talking and debating and laughing. I felt him twirling me around in his arms. I saw the future unfolding with all its mysterious promise. I saw art being part of my life but at the same time, I saw myself grounded and responsible to the people who cared about me. For the first time, I believed it could all happen.

I picked up my new guitar and started to strum.

I started writing a song and singing these words:

We're all just hanging on by a thread.
But what a thread.

ENCORE

The Call

It seemed like forever that I listened to the phone ring, and finally someone picked up. It was Maggie. I recognized her husky voice.

"Yeah," she said.

"Hi, this is Blanche Kelly. I'm wondering how you felt about my article."

She coughed and then said, "Blanche, I got your material. It's really long."

"I know. I tried to cut it down but that didn't work out."

"It's interesting."

"You read it? That's great."

"Yeah, but it's entirely too long."

"Okay."

I waited for her to tell me what to do.

She said, "Is it all true?"

"Of course."

She said, "I pitched it to my editors. We had the idea of making it a serialized piece."

"What does that mean?"

"We can't print it all at once. But we're interested in making it a serialized article—print it in parts in a couple of the magazines over a period of time. It would help if you could get us an interview with your father."

There had been a time in my life when that would have made my blood run cold. But I wasn't like that anymore.

"No can do. I don't really have access to him," I said.

"Well, without that, we really don't know what to do with this."

"Okay," I said. "Thanks anyway."

I was about to hang up. Then Maggie said, "Wait."

I waited.

She said, "It's a really good story. Have you ever thought of turning it into a book? We could publish the first chapter. That's called first serial."

"I'm a high school student. I think about grades and dates and stuff," I told her.

"Well, I understand, but this could be your really big break. You're the daughter. It's a tell-all story. Think about it."

I had thought about it already. I was having a nice summer, hanging out with Jeff and singing and writing and recording songs. There was plenty of time in my life to be great and not because of my father. I didn't need to have it right away.

I said, "Maggie, you know what? I'm just a kid. I'm

going to take the time and be one. I'm more than Duncan Kelly's daughter."

"Wait, Blanche, I can imagine how you feel but you can be a kid anytime. There are limited chances to be great."

"I think you've got that backward, Maggie."

"Do I?" she asked with raspy swagger.

"Yeah. You obviously can't imagine. See you on the other side."

"Blanche," I heard her say as I guided the phone back into the cradle. "Blanche, wait."

Blanche knew she had waited long enough. Now she was going to live.